ASPCA kids

PET RESCUE CLUB

3 Books in 1!

ASPCA kids
PET RESCUE CLUB
3 Books in 1!

by Catherine Hapka

illustrated by Dana Regan

studio fun

A READER'S DIGEST COMPANY

White Plains, New York • Montréal, Québec • Bath, United Kingdom

Cover illustration by Steve James
Photo of Lola courtesy of Geoffrey Tischman

The books in this collection were previously published individually by
Studio Fun International, Inc.

Published by Studio Fun International, Inc.
44 South Broadway, White Plains, NY 10601 U.S.A. and
Studio Fun International Limited,
The Ice House, 124-126 Walcot Street, Bath UK BA1 5BG
Illustration ©2015 Studio Fun International, Inc.
Text ©2015 ASPCA®
All rights reserved.
First edition in this format ©2016
Studio Fun Books is a trademark of Studio Fun International, Inc.,
a subsidiary of Trusted Media Brands, Inc.
Printed in the United States of America.
10 9 8 7 6 5 4 3 2 1

*The American Society for the Prevention of Cruelty to Animals (ASPCA®)
will receive a minimum guarantee from Studio Fun International, Inc. of
$25,000 for the sale of ASPCA® products
through December 2017.

Comments? Questions? Call us at: 1-888-217-3346

For all the shelter workers
who help people find their pets and pets find their people.

Contents

Contents

A New Home for Truman

by Catherine Hapka
illustrated by Dana Regan

1

The Best Birthday Ever!

"Happy birthday, Janey!" Lolli Simpson exclaimed.

Janey Whitfield set down her lunch tray at her usual spot across from Lolli. "It's not my birthday yet," she told her best friend with a smile. "Not until tomorrow, remember?"

"I know." Lolli pushed a lock of curly black hair out of her eyes. "But tomorrow is Saturday. I wanted you to be able to celebrate here at school with all your friends."

Lolli waved a hand at the other people sitting at the table. Their friend Adam Santos was next to Janey. Several kids from their fourth grade class were a little farther down, talking about that morning's spelling test.

"Come on, everybody!" Lolli called out. "Let's sing!"

She led the whole table in a round of "Happy Birthday to You." A few kids at nearby tables joined in. Janey loved every second of it. It was great having everyone sing to her!

"Thanks, everybody!" she called out when the song was finished. She waved, and some of the other kids waved back. Soon they all went back to their own conversations. "Thanks, Lolli," Janey told her friend. "That was fab." Janey loved to use interesting words whenever she could. Her favorite right then was "fab." It was short for fabulous.

"Wait—there's more." Lolli reached into her insulated lunch bag and pulled out a small reusable container. Lolli's parents liked to call themselves back-to-the-land hippies. They lived on a small farm outside of town and grew their own organic food. They bought most of their clothes at thrift stores and recycled everything. Lolli never brought brown paper bags or plastic baggies for her lunch like most of the other kids. She had a whole set of reusable bags and containers that she used instead.

"What is it?" Janey opened the container and peered at the grayish-brown lump inside.

"It's a cupcake." Lolli grinned. "Dad helped me make it just for you."

"Oh. Thanks." Janey smiled. "Um, it looks…interesting."

"That's a cupcake?" a new voice exclaimed loudly in Janey's ear.

Janey looked up. Zach Goldman had just stopped by their table. Zach was friends with Adam, but Janey didn't like him very much. He was rowdy, loud, and kind of obnoxious. Once when Janey had received the highest grade in the class on a math test, Zach had called her "Brainy Janey" for almost a month.

Zach leaned over for a better look at the cupcake. He was holding his skateboard under his arm, and the end of it poked Janey in the back.

"Ow," she said, pushing him away. "What are you doing?"

Zach grinned. "That doesn't look like a cupcake," he said. "It looks like something one of my mom's patients barfed up."

"Gross!" Janey made a face. Zach's mom

was a veterinarian. She treated most of the cats and dogs in town.

"It's a special recipe my dad made up," Lolli told Zach. "With zucchini, kale, and oatmeal. The cupcakes are actually really healthy, and totally organic, too."

"Zucchini and kale?" Zach said. "Do me a favor, Lolli. Don't make me a cupcake on my birthday."

With a grin, he hurried away.

Lolli looked worried. "Does it really look that bad?" she asked Janey. "I ate one of the cupcakes for breakfast, and I thought it was good."

Janey didn't like zucchini. But lots of the food at Lolli's house tasted better than it looked or sounded. So she forced herself to take a tiny bite of her birthday cupcake. She thought it would taste like mud, but it actually wasn't that bad.

"It's great," she said. "I love it. Thanks, Lolli, you're the best friend ever!"

Lolli looked relieved. "No, you are," she said. "So what are you going to do to celebrate your birthday tomorrow?"

That made Janey's smile get even bigger. "I can't wait until tomorrow," she said. "I'm pretty sure Mom and Dad are getting me something really special this year."

"Really? What?" Lolli was digging into her lunch bag again. While she wasn't looking, Janey nudged Adam. Then she broke off more than half of her cupcake and slipped it to him. She put a finger to her lips, and he nodded.

Adam popped the cupcake into his mouth in one big bite. He chewed and swallowed quickly. Then he gave Janey a thumbs-up.

Janey smiled gratefully. Adam was pretty skinny, but he ate a lot. And he liked almost everything, including the cafeteria's baked beans. Even Lolli's dog, Roscoe, wouldn't touch those!

Thinking about Roscoe reminded Janey of her big news. She turned back to Lolli. "I think my parents are finally getting me a dog," she said.

Lolli's head snapped up in surprise. "Huh?" she said. "But your dad is so allergic to animals."

Janey's father's allergies were the reason Janey had never had a pet, even though she was crazy about animals of all shapes and sizes. Whenever Mr. Whitfield was around any creature with fur or feathers, he started wheezing and sneezing. His eyes turned red, and his nose turned redder. He sniffled nonstop. It even happened when he was around Janey's aunt's poodle. Janey had read that poodles weren't supposed to bother people with allergies as much since they didn't shed. But her parents had explained that it didn't really work that way.

"I know. But I figured out a way to compromise," Janey told Lolli. "See, I did some research on the Internet. I found out there are allergy shots for people with animal allergies! Isn't that great?"

"Allergy shots?" Lolli looked uncertain. "You want your dad to get shots so you can have a dog?"

"Uh-huh. I printed out some articles about the allergy shots." Janey broke off a tiny piece of cupcake and ate it. "I started leaving them lying around the house about a month ago. I figured that would give Dad plenty of time to talk to his doctor about getting the shots. I also left some pictures and information about my favorite dog breeds."

"Really?" Adam looked up from his lunch. "What breeds did you pick?"

Adam was very interested in dogs. Even though he was only nine, he'd been running his own successful pet-sitting business for over a year. He fed and walked people's dogs for them after school and any other time they needed him. He also helped people train their dogs sometimes. He'd taught Roscoe how to shake hands and balance a dog treat on his nose.

"I was thinking about a Maltese or a papillon," Janey told him. "They both seem really cute and fun. And I thought maybe a small dog like that would mean Dad needs to get the shots less often."

Adam nodded. "I walked a Maltese once.

I liked her."

Lolli laughed. "You like every dog you walk, Adam," she said. Then she turned to Janey. "Maybe you don't need a fancy breed. What's wrong with a nice all-American mutt like Roscoe?"

"That would be fine, too. Roscoe is totally fab," Janey said. She meant it, too. Roscoe was a big, lovable goof who had come from the local animal shelter as a puppy. He was part rottweiler, part Labrador retriever, and part who-knew-what. Janey had spent many happy hours at Lolli's place playing fetch with Roscoe, swimming with him in the pond, or just lying in the grass rubbing his belly.

"I bet you could find a dog just as great as Roscoe at the Third Street Animal Shelter,"

Lolli said. "The dogs and cats there all really need homes. My parents and I go there sometimes to volunteer. Actually, Mom said we might go tomorrow to drop off some homemade dog and cat toys we made last weekend. I could help you look at dogs then if you want."

"That would be awesome," Janey said. "I'll mention it to my parents if they haven't gotten my dog yet. Come to think of it, they might be thinking the same thing. They donate money to the shelter every year." She sighed happily. "Anyway, I don't really care what kind of dog I get. I just can't wait to have one of my very own!"

She'd been dreaming about this day ever since she could remember. Janey had always loved animals—all animals. She read books about dogs, hung cute pictures of cats on her walls, and doodled horses and elephants and rabbits all over the margins of her school notebooks. She loved spending time with Roscoe, Adam's dog-sitting clients, and any other animal that came along. But nothing would compare to having a pet of her very own, to cuddle and snuggle with any time she wanted.

It was going to be so great! She shivered with excitement, wondering how she was ever going to wait until tomorrow.

2

Birthday Surprises

Janey woke up early the next morning. For a second she couldn't remember why she was excited. Then she smiled.

"Happy birthday to me!" she said, jumping out of bed.

She pulled on her bathrobe and raced downstairs. The smell of banana pancakes and bacon greeted her.

"Happy birthday, sweetheart!" Janey's father sang out. He was at the stove with a spatula. "I'm making your favorite breakfast."

"Thanks, Daddy." Janey looked around the kitchen. There was a pile of wrapped gifts on the counter. None of the packages had air holes that she could see.

But she couldn't see her mother, either. Maybe Mom was out in the garage with the dog, waiting to surprise her.

Then her mother hurried in from the living room. "Happy birthday, Janey, love!" she said. "How does it feel to be a year older?"

"Fab," Janey said. Her father set a platter of pancakes and bacon in front of her, and Janey helped herself. "I can't wait to see what you got me this year!"

Her parents traded a smile. "We can't wait, either," Janey's father said. "Eat your birthday breakfast, and then you can open your gifts."

Janey loved banana pancakes and bacon. But that morning, she hardly tasted them. She ate as fast as she could.

"Finished!" she said, gulping down some juice. "Time for presents."

Her parents both laughed. "All right," her mother said. "Go ahead, love."

Janey grabbed one of the gifts and shook it. Even if there wasn't a dog in the pile of gifts, maybe the packages contained dog stuff, like a collar and leash or food dishes or dog toys. Now that she thought about it, that made more sense anyway. Then Janey would be all ready to go and pick out her own dog at the shelter. She couldn't wait!

She ripped the paper off the first gift. "Oh," she said in surprise.

There was no collar or leash. No dishes or dog toys, either. Just a shirt with a sparkly collar.

"It's the one you liked at the mall last weekend, remember?" her mother said with a smile.

Janey nodded. She did like the shirt, even if she wasn't that excited about it right now. But maybe she could wear it to the shelter when she chose her dog.

"Thanks," she said. "Next!"

For a second she thought the next gift was a collar, but then she realized it was a bracelet. Janey opened several more packages after that, but all of them contained non-dog gifts.

Finally there was only one gift left. That had to be the dog gift!

Janey picked it up. "Don't shake that one, sweetheart," her father said.

Janey nodded. She had a bad feeling about this. The shape and weight of the gift didn't seem right for any kind of dog stuff. It was light and rectangular.

She opened it quickly. "Oh," she said. "A tablet computer."

"This model just came out last week." Her father sounded excited. "We knew you'd love it!"

Her mother nodded. "Your laptop is getting old," she explained. "This will be so much better."

"It's already fully loaded, too," her father said. "It's got a great browser, a kid-safe blogging platform, and of course all your favorite games—like Puppy Playtime."

Janey perked up. "Puppy Playtime?" she echoed with a smile. "Yes, I do love that game."

She paused, waiting for her parents to say something else about puppies—like that they were taking Janey to get one! But her father just went on talking about the other software on the tablet.

"What's wrong, love?" Janey's mother interrupted her husband. "You don't look as excited as we expected."

Janey bit her lip. Were her parents teasing her? That didn't seem like them.

"What about my dog?" she blurted out.

"Dog?" Janey's mother traded a look with Janey's father.

"Oh, Janey." Her father shook his head. "Is this about those printouts I found on my desk a couple of weeks ago?"

Janey nodded. "Did you read them? All you need to do is get a few shots and you won't be allergic to animals anymore!"

"I'm afraid it's not that simple," Janey's mother said. "We looked into the shots once, but the doctor advised against it because your father has mild asthma."

Janey couldn't believe that this was happening. She felt her face turning red. If she didn't get away, she'd start crying or yelling—probably both.

"I...I need to call Lolli," she choked out. "I think she wants me to come to her house."

Her mother looked worried. "Are you sure? We were going to watch a movie, or—"

Mr. Whitfield put a hand on his wife's arm. "It's okay, Janey," he said softly. "Go ahead and call Lolli. We can watch that movie later."

There was no answer on the phone at Lolli's farmhouse, so Janey called Lolli's mom's cell phone. It turned out that the whole family was in the car on their way to the shelter.

"We're just five minutes from your house," Mrs. Simpson told Janey. "We'll swing by and pick you up. I know you love visiting the animals at the shelter."

"Thanks," Janey said.

While her father cleared the breakfast dishes and her mother picked up the wrapping paper from her gifts, Janey ran upstairs to change out of her pajamas. Then she stood in the front hall until she saw the Simpsons' battered old station wagon pull to the curb in front of her house.

"Lolli's parents are here to pick me up," she called. "I'll be back in a while."

Ten minutes later, she was walking into the Third Street Animal Shelter with Lolli and her parents. Mr. Simpson was carrying a hemp bag filled with homemade dog and cat toys. Mrs. Simpson had a bag of organic kale from her garden. She'd explained that it was for some pet rabbits that had come into the shelter that week.

The shelter was a one-story brick building tucked between the post office and a florist shop. Inside, the lobby was painted with cheerful murals of cats, dogs, and other animals. The muffled sound of barking came from beyond a door marked Dog Room.

"I expected to come here today," Janey said sadly, staring at that door. "But I thought it would be to pick out my own dog."

Mrs. Simpson put her arm around Janey's shoulder. During the ride over, Janey had told Lolli and her parents what had happened.

A young woman came out from behind the front desk and hurried over. She was in her twenties, with a blond ponytail and a bright smile. "Oh, you brought the toys!" she exclaimed. "Thanks so much—I know the critters will love them."

"You're welcome, Kitty," Mrs. Simpson said.

That made Janey smile. "You work in an animal shelter, and your name is Kitty?" she asked the young woman.

Kitty laughed. "Actually, it's Kathleen," she said. "But after I smuggled a whole litter of kittens into my room as a kid, my family started calling me Kitty. And I guess it stuck!"

"It's Janey's birthday today," Mr. Simpson told Kitty. "Can she play with some animals to help her celebrate?"

"Of course!" Kitty said. "Go on into the Meet and Greet Room, and I'll bring somebody in for you to play with. Would you prefer cats or dogs?"

"I love both," Janey said. "But I especially like dogs, I guess."

She followed Lolli through a doorway across from the front desk. Inside was a small room with a tile floor. There were benches and beanbag chairs, as well as several scratching posts and a bucket filled with toys and treats.

Soon Kitty returned. She was leading two half-grown puppies. One was a small terrier mix, and the other was a tall, gangly brown dog whose fringed tail never stopped wagging.

"This is Buster, and this is Lyle," Kitty said. "They're both super friendly and playful. Go ahead and wear them out if you can— you'll be doing me a favor!" She laughed and left, pulling the door shut behind her.

"Oh, you're adorable!" Janey exclaimed, falling to her knees and cuddling the puppies. For a second she felt happy, like she always did when animals were around. But she felt sad at the same time. She would love to take home either Buster or Lyle—or better yet, both of them! But that wasn't going to happen.

"They're so cute!" Lolli exclaimed, giggling as Lyle licked her chin. "I bet Roscoe would love a couple of puppies to play with!"

"Don't even think about it," her mother said with a laugh. "One dog is more than enough for this family."

"Oh, well." Lolli smiled. "At least I can play with them here." She turned to Janey. "That gives me a great idea. Why don't we volunteer here at the shelter together? They let kids help out if their parents sign a form. We could come once or twice a week after school."

"That sounds fun," Janey agreed. "Not as much fun as having my own pet, but better than nothing." She hugged Buster as he wiggled onto her lap. "A puppy would be a lot cuddlier than some stupid old tablet."

"I know," Lolli agreed. "Your tablet sounds cool, though. Does it take pictures? Too bad you didn't bring it with you, or I could take some photos of you with Buster and Lyle."

"Yeah." Janey tickled Buster under his furry chin. "But wait—that gives me a totally fab idea…"

3

Janey's Big Idea

Half an hour later, the Simpsons dropped Janey and Lolli off at Janey's house. Janey rushed inside. "Mom! Daddy!" she yelled. "Where are you?"

Her mother came into the front hall from the kitchen. "Hello, Lolli," she said. "Janey, you look like you're in a better mood than when you left."

"I'm sorry about earlier," Janey said, hurrying over to give her mother a hug. "You too, Daddy," she added as her father wandered in carrying a news magazine. "I loved all my presents, even if none of them is a dog."

"Good, good." Her father looked relieved. "I'm sorry we can't get a pet, sweetheart."

"I know. But listen, I had a great idea that might be the next best thing," Janey said.

Her mother smiled. "Uh-oh," she said. "What is it—a robot dog?"

Lolli giggled. "That definitely sounds like something Janey would invent!"

Janey giggled, too. "Maybe someday. But my great idea does involve technology— namely, my awesome new tablet!" The tablet was still on the table where she'd left it. She hurried over and picked it up. "You said this has a blogging program, right?"

"Yes," her father said. "It's a brand new platform made specifically for bloggers under fourteen. There are all kinds of safety features, and—"

"Perfect," Janey interrupted. "Because that's my idea. I'm going to start a blog! It'll be called, um, Janey's Pet Place, and kids can use it to share cute pictures of their cats and dogs and other pets."

"What a wonderful idea, love!" her mother said.

"I know." Janey smiled. "That way, it'll be like I have all the pets in town around me all the time!" She grabbed Lolli's hand. "Come on, I can't wait—let's go up to my room and figure out how to get started!"

An hour later, Janey was feeling both excited and frustrated. "The text we wrote is perfect," she told Lolli, "but it won't do any good if we can't figure out how to get the blog set up the way I want it!"

"I know, right?" Lolli poked at the tablet's on-screen keypad. "If this blog thingy is made for kids, shouldn't it be easy to use?"

Janey pulled the tablet closer again and tried—again—to load the text into the box she'd just finished creating. It looked really cool, with a border of frolicking puppies and kittens and a background of clouds. But when she hit the enter key, all she got in return was an annoying error message—again.

"Aargh!" she cried. "I want to get it working already so I can start getting cute pet photos!"

A bark drifted in through the window. "Maybe that dog outside wants to be on your blog," Lolli joked. "He's telling you to hurry up!"

Janey hopped off her bed and went to the window. A cute golden retriever was sniffing the bushes along the sidewalk. A familiar figure was holding the dog's leash.

"Hey, it's Adam!" Janey told Lolli. "He's walking one of his dog-sitting clients. Let's go ask him if he knows how to work the blog software."

"Adam?" Lolli sounded dubious. "He's not that interested in computers—just dogs."

Janey tucked her tablet under her arm and headed for the door. "Still, he's smart, right?" she said. "Maybe he can figure out what we're doing wrong. Besides, I love that golden retriever he's walking right now—I want to go out and pet him."

Lolli smiled. "In that case, what are we waiting for?"

The big, friendly dog greeted Janey and Lolli happily. So did Adam. But he shook his head as he studied the blog screen.

"Sorry, guys," he said. "I have no clue. Maybe you should ask Zach. He's practically a technology genius."

"Zach? Really?" Now it was Janey's turn to be doubtful. She didn't think Zach was good at anything except being totally obnoxious!

"Uh-huh." Adam bent down to untangle the leash from around the golden retriever's leg. "He helped my parents set up a photo-sharing site last year so my relatives can all see pictures of my little sisters and me. And he's always fixing the computer his dad uses for work. I bet a blogging site will be no problem for him."

"It's worth a try," Lolli said. "Zach lives

near here, doesn't he?"

"He's on the next block," Janey said. She frowned at Adam. "Are you sure he's good with computer stuff? What if he wrecks my new tablet?"

"He won't," Adam said. "Trust me, he can get your blog working if anyone can."

Janey sighed. "Fine," she said. "I guess we can go see if he's home. I'd do just about anything to get my blog started!"

4
Going Live

"There he is," Lolli said as the girls turned the corner onto Zach's block.

Janey saw him, too. Zach was in front of his house. He was messing around with his skateboard, trying to get it to jump over a big crack in the sidewalk.

"Hi," Janey said, hurrying up to him. "What are you doing?"

"Learning Chinese," Zach said with a smirk. "What does it look like?"

Janey looked at the house. Loud music was coming out of an open window. "Is someone having a party?"

"Nah, that's just my older brothers." Zach rolled his eyes. "A bunch of their dumb friends came over. They're lucky my dad is the only one home. My mom would never let them play their stupid music so loud."

"Where's your mom?" Lolli asked.

Zach flipped his skateboard up, catching it in one hand. "At work. Her clinic is open on Saturdays."

"Oh." Janey thought it was so cool that Zach's mom was a veterinarian. That was practically her dream job! She didn't say that, though. She figured Zach would probably just make fun of her. "Listen, Adam says you're good at computers...."

She and Lolli told him about all the problems they were having. When Janey held out her tablet, Zach's eyes lit up.

"Cool!" he exclaimed. "I've been dying to get one of these!" Then his face fell. "I probably won't, though. My parents say one computer is enough for the whole family to share."

"We only have one computer, too," Lolli told him.

Zach grinned. "Yeah, but that's because your parents are weirdos," he teased her.

"They are not!" Janey retorted with a frown.

But Lolli just laughed. "It's okay. Mom and Dad call themselves weirdos all the time. So Zach, do you think you can help us with the blog?"

"Duh, that's easy." Zach sat down on his skateboard with the tablet on his lap. His fingers flew over the keypad.

"What are you doing?" Janey couldn't help being a little nervous. What if Zach broke her new tablet? Then she'd have to wait until she got it fixed to start her blog.

Zach didn't answer for a second. Finally he looked up and grinned. "There," he said, showing Janey the screen. "Is that all you needed me to do?"

Janey gasped. The blog looked perfect! The text was exactly where it was supposed to be. Zach had cropped and resized the photos of cats and dogs Janey had pasted onto the page, too. She hadn't asked him to do that, but the photos looked better, so she didn't complain.

"Awesome!" she said. "Thanks, you really…"

She cut herself off with a gasp. Something was happening on the screen. As Janey stared in horror, the edges of her blog page seemed to peel back. Then a cartoon dinosaur leaped into view and started chomping on the text box!

"Hey!" she cried while Zach started laughing so hard he almost fell off his skateboard. "You did that on purpose, didn't you?"

"No, it must be a virus or something." Zach was laughing so hard he could barely get the words out. "You should see your face, Janey!"

Lolli giggled. "That's pretty funny, Zach," she said. "How'd you do it?"

"I could tell you, but you wouldn't understand." Zach grinned. "Cool, right?"

"No." Janey was still frowning. "Fix it!"

"Okay, okay." Zach rolled his eyes. "Next birthday, make sure you ask for a sense of humor, okay?"

Lolli smiled at Janey. "Come on, it was a little bit funny, right?" Lolli said in her soothing way. "Besides, I'm sure Zach is going to fix it right now. Right, Zach?"

"Right." Zach was already bent over the tablet again.

Janey was tempted to grab it away from him. But she decided to give Zach one more chance.

And ten minutes later, she was glad. Zach got rid of the dinosaur and adjusted a few other things. Now the blog looked perfect!

"There," Zach said, pressing a key on-screen. "You're live. Kids should be able to see the blog now."

"Thanks, Zach!" Janey took her tablet back and smiled at the screen. "I can't wait for the cute pet pictures to start coming in!"

"How's the blog going, sweetheart?" Janey's father asked the next day as Janey helped him clear the lunch dishes.

"Fab." Janey dropped a handful of silverware into the dishwasher. Then she hurried back to the table and picked up her tablet. "People are already posting tons of awesome pictures! This one's my favorite so far."

She scrolled down and showed him a

photo of an adorable black-and-white cat leaping at a butterfly. Her father chuckled.

"Very cute," he agreed. He checked his watch. "Ready to head over to Lolli's? I want to be back here before the game starts on TV."

Janey nodded. She'd made plans to spend Sunday afternoon over at Lolli's house so they could write the next blog entry together. Janey was planning to post every few days with her thoughts about animals and anything else she could think of to write about. She was also going to choose her favorite photos in several categories—cutest pet, funniest pose, best action shot, and other stuff like that. She figured that would encourage people to keep sending photos.

It took about ten minutes to drive to Lolli's farm on the edge of town. Soon the Whitfields' car was bumping and jangling up the Simpsons' long gravel driveway. There was an orchard on one side, and a pasture on the other with two goats and a sheep in it. Usually Janey liked to stop and say hello to the animals, but today she just waved at them as the car passed.

"Have fun," her father said as he stopped in front of the Simpsons' two-story, pointy-roofed farmhouse. The wooden porch sagged a little, and a small flock of chickens was pecking at the dandelions growing on the front lawn. It was very different from the Whitfields' tidy suburban home. But Janey thought the farmhouse was beautiful. She and Lolli had helped

Mrs. Simpson paint the shutters a gorgeous shade of sky blue. And everywhere she looked, something was blooming.

As Janey climbed out of the car, the front door opened. Roscoe bounded out, barking happily.

"Hey, buddy!" Janey greeted Roscoe as he almost crashed into her.

Lolli was right behind Roscoe. She waved to Janey's father as he drove away. Then she grabbed Roscoe by the collar and pulled him away from Janey.

"Leave her alone, Roscoe," she said. "You'll make her drop her tablet!"

"Don't worry, I'm holding on tight," Janey said with a laugh. "Ready to see more cute pictures?"

Just then the tablet let out a ping. "Ooh!" Lolli said. "Does that mean someone else just posted a photo?"

"Uh-huh. We should try to guess what kind of animal it will be this time," Janey said, holding her hand over the screen. "I'll guess that it's a fluffy long-haired cat."

"I guess it's, um, a cute potbelly pig," Lolli said with a giggle.

"And the answer is…" Janey moved her hand and looked.

Then she gasped. The picture wasn't of a cat, or of a potbelly pig, either. It wasn't anything cute at all.

It showed a cowering, matted, skinny little gray dog chained in a bare yard.

5

Search and Rescue

"Oh, it's horrible!" Janey blurted out. She wished she hadn't seen the photo at all. The dog looked miserable. He had floppy ears and big, brown eyes. Other than that, he was so dirty and dusty that Janey couldn't even guess what kind of dog he was.

Lolli's eyes filled with tears. "Who would treat a dog like that?" she cried. "We have to do something!"

"What can we do?" Janey rubbed Roscoe's head.

"Let's go ask Mom and Dad." Lolli grabbed the tablet and hurried into the house.

The inside of the farmhouse smelled like scented candles, coffee, and Roscoe. Lolli's parents were sitting at the big wooden kitchen table drinking coffee and reading the Sunday newspaper.

When Lolli showed them the picture,

her mother looked concerned. "Oh, the poor thing," she said.

Lolli's father ran a hand through his curly hair. "Where did this photo come from, girls?" he asked.

"I'm not sure." Janey shrugged. "Whoever sent it didn't put her name on it."

"What can we do to help that dog?" Lolli asked her parents.

Mr. and Mrs. Simpson glanced at each other. "That's our girl," Mr. Simpson said. "'The only thing necessary for evil to triumph is for good men to do nothing.'"

"Huh?" Janey blinked. Was Lolli's dad going crazy, or did he think she and Lolli were men?

"It's a famous quotation," Mrs. Simpson explained with a smile. "It means we're very proud of you two for wanting to get involved."

Lolli's father nodded. "Why don't you forward that photo to the animal shelter?" he suggested. "The people there will know how to get the authorities on the case."

"Good idea." Janey found the shelter's website. She forwarded the photo of the skinny dog to the e-mail address on the contact page.

"I hope they can help that dog," Lolli said softly, staring at the photo.

Janey glanced at it one more time, then shuddered and clicked it off. She didn't want to look at the poor little dog's sad face any longer.

"Let's look at some nicer pictures now," she said.

But it didn't work. Janey couldn't stop thinking about the sad gray dog for the rest of the day.

⁓

"I can't stand it any longer," Janey told Lolli the next day at recess. "I'm going to ask Ms. Tanaka if I can call the shelter."

"Good idea," Lolli agreed.

Their homeroom teacher, Ms. Tanaka, was the playground monitor that day. Janey was glad it was her and not grumpy old Mr. Wells. Ms. Tanaka was young and wore cool clothes and laughed a lot.

"Oh, wow," Ms. Tanaka said when she heard about the neglected dog. "Go ahead and check in with the shelter. Here—you can use my phone."

"Thanks." Janey took the phone the teacher handed her.

"Third Street Animal Shelter, may I help you?" a familiar-sounding voice answered when Janey called the shelter's number.

"Kitty? Is that you?" Janey said. She told the shelter worker who she was and why she was calling.

"Oh, I'm so glad you checked in, Janey," Kitty replied. "Do you know anything else about the dog in that photo?"

"No." Janey clutched the phone tighter. "That's why I sent it to you guys. That dog needs help!"

"Oh, yes, we agree." Kitty sounded apologetic. "We forwarded the photo to the town's animal control officer. But she can't take action since nobody knows where the dog is located. If you can find out more, please call us back, okay?"

"Um, okay." Janey wasn't sure how Kitty expected her to find out more. She was just a kid!

She hung up the phone and gave it back to Ms. Tanaka. The teacher was listening to a third grader complain about a boy teasing her, so she just nodded and smiled.

Then Janey went back over to Lolli and told her what Kitty had said. "Now what?" Janey finished. "We have to figure out how to help that dog!"

"Yes, definitely," Lolli agreed, looking worried. She glanced toward the playing field, where several kids were kicking a soccer ball around. "Adam's over there. Let's see if he has any ideas."

They called Adam over, showed him the dog's picture, and told him what was going on. "Wow," he said with a frown. "That's messed up. How can anyone keep a dog that way?"

"Have you ever seen this dog?" Janey asked him. "You know—while you're out walking dogs and stuff?"

"No way." Adam shook his head. "I'd definitely remember!"

Janey bit her lip. Adam walked dogs all over town. "What if that dog isn't even around here?" she wondered. "It could come from a town miles away. Then we'll never find—hey, watch it!"

Zach was zooming straight toward her on his skateboard. He stopped just in time to avoid crashing into her.

"Hey." He grinned. "I didn't scare you, did I? So how's the blog business?"

Janey didn't answer. She wished Zach

would go away. But Lolli and Adam started telling him about the skinny dog.

"…but we don't know where the dog is, so they can't help him," Lolli finished.

"No problem." Zach grabbed Janey's tablet out of her hand. "I can find out who sent the photo. Then all you have to do is track him down and ask where he saw the dog."

"You can?" Adam brightened. "How?"

Zach was already typing on the keypad. "You need to have a verified name and address to post on the blog," he mumbled as he worked. "It's part of the kid-safe software." He hit one more key. "Here you go—this is who sent that picture."

"Vanessa Chaudhry," Lolli read aloud. Her eyes widened. "Hey, she goes to this school!"

Janey knew Vanessa, too. She was the best singer in the fifth grade—she always had solos in the school concerts. "The fifth graders should be coming out for recess while we're on our way in," Janey said. "Let's try to talk to her then."

Vanessa looked startled when Janey and the others surrounded her a few minutes later. At first she tried to deny she'd taken the picture. But when Janey told her that the animal shelter couldn't help the dog without more information, Vanessa bit her lip.

"Oh! I thought posting the picture

would be enough," she said. "I really want someone to rescue that poor dog."

"Then tell us where he is!" Janey urged. "We won't tell anyone you told us."

"Okay." Vanessa described where she'd seen the dog. It was a rural area on the opposite side of town from Lolli's farm. "I really hope you can help him," Vanessa added as Ms. Tanaka headed over to shoo Janey and her classmates inside. "No dog should have to live like that."

6

Truman Is Safe!

"They got him!" Janey cried, bursting out of the school's main office.

It was the next afternoon. Mr. Wells had dismissed the class a few minutes earlier. Janey had run straight to the office so she could use the phone there to call the shelter.

"Hip hip hooray!" Lolli cheered, jumping up and down. "What did Kitty say?"

"The animal control officer went out yesterday and talked to the dog's owners," Janey said. She and Lolli wandered down the hall toward the school exit. "They agreed to give the dog to the shelter. He's there now!"

"We should go see him!" Lolli grabbed Janey's arm. "Let's call home and see if our parents will let us walk over to the shelter."

They turned around and rushed back to the office. They got there at the same time as Ms. Tanaka.

"Everything okay, girls?" the teacher asked.

"Yes," Janey replied. "We just need to use the phone."

Ms. Tanaka nodded and held the door open for them. Then the teacher went to check her office mail cubby as the girls headed toward the desk to ask the secretary for permission to use the phone.

"You can call first," Janey told Lolli.

Lolli's father gave permission right away.

But when Janey called home, her mother sounded reluctant. "Maybe you should come home first," she said. "I can drive you and Lolli to the shelter."

"Please, Mom. We don't want to wait that long. Besides, the shelter is only a few blocks from school," Janey said. "Lolli's parents already said yes."

"That's right, Mrs. Whitfield," Lolli said, leaning over Janey's shoulder to talk into the phone. "We'll be careful, we promise!"

"Did I hear you girls say you're going to the Third Street Shelter?" Ms. Tanaka asked, walking over.

"Maybe," Janey said. "If I can talk my mom into saying yes."

Ms. Tanaka smiled. "If it helps, you can tell her I'll walk there with you," she offered. "I was thinking about heading over there myself."

Her offer did help. Janey's mother finally said it was okay. Soon Janey, Lolli, and Ms. Tanaka were walking down the sidewalk toward Third Street.

"Why are you going to the shelter?" Lolli asked her teacher.

Ms. Tanaka chuckled. "Actually, you guys inspired me. I just moved to a new apartment last month, and this one allows pets. I've been thinking about getting a dog, and hearing you talk about the shelter made me decide it's time to start looking for the perfect best friend."

"That's awesome!" For a second, Janey was envious. It seemed everyone could have a pet except her! Then she had a great idea. "I know—you should adopt the dog we saved!"

"Hmm. I like the idea of rescuing a dog that really needs me." Ms. Tanaka sounded interested. "What does he look like?"

Janey showed her the picture from her blog. "He looks kind of bad here," she said. "But I bet all he needs is a good brushing and some food and he'll be supercute!"

"Oh, he's cute—but awfully small. I was thinking about a bigger dog." Ms. Tanaka smiled. "See, I had horses growing up, so I'm used to big pets. A really huge dog is the next best thing to a horse!"

Lolli laughed, while Janey smiled weakly. "Are you sure you don't want him?" she asked.

"Sorry." Ms. Tanaka patted her arm. "But don't worry—your dog is adorable. I'm sure he'll find a home fast."

When they reached the shelter, Ms. Tanaka said good-bye and headed into the dog room. Meanwhile, Kitty rushed over to greet the girls.

"I'm so glad you came!" she said. "Stay right here, and I'll go get Truman so he can thank you in person!"

"Truman?" Janey echoed.

"That's the dog you saved. He's a real sweetie." Kitty smiled. "Be right back."

Moments later she returned with a dog on a leash. Janey barely recognized him from his picture! Someone had given him a bath, brushed the tangles out of his silky fur, and trimmed the hair on his ears and paws.

Janey had memorized every breed from her dog books, and she thought Truman looked as if he might be a cross between a schnauzer and a shih tzu. Whatever he was, he was one of the cutest dogs she'd ever seen!

"Oh, you're so adorable!" she cried, reaching for him.

Truman ducked away from her touch, but he wagged his short tail and pricked up his ears with curiosity. "You'll have to take it easy and be patient with him," Kitty advised. "He's still a little shy. But he's very sweet once he trusts you. Come on—let's hang out in the Meet and Greet room so you can all get to know each other."

They all went into the small room. Truman sniffed everything carefully, then flopped down on one of the beanbag chairs. Meanwhile Kitty told the girls what the animal officer had found out.

"Truman belonged to an elderly man who adored him," she said. "Then the owner died, and Truman went to live with the man's relatives. But one of the kids in the house was allergic."

"Just like Janey's dad," Lolli said.

Janey nodded. "The family stuck him outside and kind of forgot about him, I guess. One of the other kids was supposed to feed him and give him water but he didn't always remember."

Janey clenched her fists. "How could anyone be so horrible?" she exclaimed. "Especially with a sweet dog like Truman!"

"Try not to think about it," Lolli advised. "He's safe now, and I'm sure somebody great will adopt him."

"I wish I could adopt him," Janey said.

Lolli gave her a sympathetic smile. "Try not to think about that, either."

Janey tried. For the next hour, she and Lolli stayed with Truman. He was shy at first, but eventually he seemed to decide the girls were okay. After that, they could hardly get him to stop playing!

Janey was disappointed when her mother arrived to pick them up. "We'll come visit you again soon, Truman," she promised the little dog.

"Right," Lolli agreed. "Unless someone adopts you before that!"

"I'm sure it won't take long." Janey smiled and rubbed Truman's silky ears. She giggled as the little dog licked her from her chin to her forehead. "Who could resist a face—or a tongue—like that?"

7

Still Waiting

"Did you call the shelter last night?" Lolli asked when Janey walked into school on Thursday morning.

Janey nodded and sighed. "He's still there."

"I don't get it." Lolli leaned against the wall of cubbies, watching as Janey put her stuff away. "Truman is such a great dog! Why doesn't anyone want to take him home?"

"I have no idea." Janey was about to put her tablet in the cubby with the rest of her things. Then she stopped and stared at it. "But I just thought of something. My blog was what saved Truman, right? Maybe it can also help him find the perfect home!"

"What do you mean?" Lolli asked.

Janey was already logging on to the Internet. "I'm going to post an update about Truman. Lots of people saw the picture of him on my blog."

"That's true," Lolli agreed. "You got tons of comments about how horrible he looked."

"So now I'll tell everyone he's safe and looking for a home." Janey typed quickly, describing how the animal officer had saved Truman. She added that the little dog was at the shelter waiting for an adopter to come and take him home.

Lolli watched over her shoulder. "Don't forget to mention how cute he looks now that he's healthy and clean," she suggested.

Janey nodded. She wished she'd taken pictures of Truman at the shelter. Maybe she could get some later. But her words would have to do for now.

"There!" she said, hitting the key to post the blurb. "That should do the trick."

But when Janey called the shelter again on Saturday, Kitty told her that Truman was still there.

"Your ad *did* work, though," Kitty added. "Sort of, anyway. Three different people came in looking for Truman because they'd seen him on your blog."

"Really? Then why is he still there?" Janey asked.

"They all decided he wasn't quite right for them," Kitty said. "They all chose different dogs instead."

"Oh." Janey sighed. "Oh, well, lots of people come to get new pets on the weekend, right? Someone will probably take him home soon. Lolli and I will be right over— we want to see him again before he finds his new owners."

Soon the two friends were at the shelter playing with Truman. A family was in the Meet and Greet room getting to know a few of the shelter's cats, so the girls tossed a rubber bone for Truman in the wide, rubber-paved aisle of the dog room. There were dogs in the runs on either side of the aisle, but Truman paid little attention to them, staying focused on the girls.

"Good boy!" Janey exclaimed when Truman pounced on the bone and then brought it back to her. "You already know how to fetch!"

"He's supersmart." said Lolli as she ruffled Truman's ears. "Aren't you, boy?"

Just then the door to the dog room opened. Kitty walked in, followed by a nicely dressed man and woman and a five-year-old boy.

"Excuse me, girls," Kitty said. "This lovely family has come to see Truman."

"That's right." The mother had a nice smile. "Are you Janey? We saw what you wrote about Truman on your blog, and we just had to meet him!"

Her husband nodded. "We were planning to get a dog this weekend anyway, and we think Truman might be perfect. Is that him?"

"Yes, this is Truman." Janey saw that Truman was backing away from the man. "Um, he's a little shy with new people."

"He's cute! Here, Truman!" The little boy rushed toward Truman, who quickly sidled out of reach.

"Slow down, son," his father called. "You don't want to startle him."

He strode over and grabbed Truman before the little dog could get away. "Careful," Kitty warned. "He's still getting used to things here, and…"

"Easy, fella! We just want to pet you, that's all." The man hugged Truman to his chest. Truman struggled against his grip, looking anxious.

"Why don't you let me hold him for you?" Janey said quickly. "He knows me, so that will help him relax."

"Ow!" the man said as Truman scrabbled against his chest, looking frantic now. "Oh, no! He just put a hole in my new shirt!"

He set Truman down and peered down at his golf shirt. Truman darted behind Janey and pressed himself against her legs. She could feel him trembling.

"It's just a shirt, Steve," the man's wife said, rolling her eyes. "But perhaps Truman isn't quite right for us after all. We don't want a dog we need to tiptoe around."

The little boy already seemed to have forgotten all about Truman. He was over by one of the runs, reaching in to pet a friendly hound mix.

"I want this one!" he cried. "Look—he likes me!"

"Can we meet that one?" the man asked
Kitty. "He seems like a good family dog."

Kitty shot Truman an anxious glance.
"Sure, let's take him over to the Meet and
Greet," she said. "I think the cats are out of
there now."

As soon as the family had disappeared,

along with Kitty and the hound mix, Truman came out of hiding. He grabbed the rubber bone and dropped it at Lolli's feet, wagging his tail.

Janey sighed. "Oh, Truman," she said, kneeling down to give the dog a hug. "You're such a sweetie pie. Why can't anyone but us see that?"

8

A Plan for Truman

A little while later, Kitty returned. "Well, at least Chance found a new home," she said, gesturing at the empty run where the hound mix had been. "That family loved him, and it was totally mutual. I think it's a great match." She bent to pat Truman, who was sniffing at her shoe. "I just wish this little guy would find his perfect match."

"Me, too," Janey said. "I can't believe nobody wants him!"

Kitty sighed. "I know. Poor Truman was just a little too shy or a little too untrained for all the people who were interested in him so far."

Just then the door opened again. Zach burst into the dog room, followed by his mother. "Yo, Truman!" Zach exclaimed loudly when he spotted the dog. "Are these girls bothering you, little guy?"

He rushed over to the dog. Janey expected Truman to try to get away, but instead he barked and jumped up on Zach's legs. Zach laughed and rubbed Truman's ears.

"Hey, he's being friendly now," Lolli said.

"Sure he is, he's my buddy." Zach grabbed the rubber bone and tossed it. Truman barked and leaped off to retrieve it.

Dr. Goldman chuckled. "Don't even think about asking again to take him home," she warned Zach. She glanced at the girls. "Zach was with me when I did Truman's intake checkup and shots the other day. As you can see, the two of them hit it off."

"Is that why you two stopped by?" Kitty asked the vet with a grin. "To adopt Truman?"

"Actually, I stopped by to take that new cat's stitches out. Seeing Truman is a bonus, but I'm afraid we can't take him home. We already have a cat, which is about all I can handle with four boys, a busy vet practice, and an absentminded husband who gets so caught up in his work that he's not likely to remember to walk a dog unless it's actually piddling on his foot." She smiled at Janey and Lolli. "Is one of you thinking about adopting Truman?"

"Our parents won't let us take him home, either," Janey said. "And nobody else seems interested, even though he's so fab!"

"Poor Truman." Lolli patted Truman as he trotted past with the rubber bone. "He just needs someone who understands him."

"Maybe." Dr. Goldman pushed Truman down gently as he dropped the bone, barked, and jumped up on her legs. "But he could also use a little training and socializing to make him more adoptable."

"What do you mean?" Janey asked.

"He's a nice dog," the vet said. "But some adopters might not be able to see the diamond in the rough the way we can." She smiled at Janey and Lolli. "If you girls want to help him find a home, maybe you can work with him a little. Teach him a few basic commands, and get him more used to being around people."

"We can do that!" Janey felt a surge of hope. "Right, Lolli?"

"Definitely!" Lolli agreed.

"Yeah," Zach put in. "I can help if you want."

"Thanks, but that's okay," Janey told him. "We've got it covered. Come on Lolli, let's start right now!"

Kitty smiled apologetically. "Actually, you'll need to get your parents to sign our volunteer form before you can do any real training or take him for walks outside," she said. "Sorry. I probably shouldn't even have let you spend all this time with him before doing that."

Janey frowned, feeling impatient. But Lolli nodded. "We can do that," she said. "We were planning to ask about volunteering here anyway, and both our parents already said it was okay, so I'm sure they'll sign. I'll call my mom to come get us, and then we'll be back as soon as we have the forms filled out and signed."

"You girls are lucky that this shelter lets kids volunteer," Dr. Goldman told them with a smile. "I would've loved to get involved like that as a kid, but the shelter in the town where I grew up only allows people over eighteen to handle the animals."

"Not here," Kitty said cheerfully. "We've found that younger kids are great with the animals! Come on, girls—let's get you those forms."

Over the next week, Janey went to the shelter as often as she could to work with Truman. Lolli usually came, too. Even Adam took some time out of his busy dog-walking schedule to show the girls some training techniques. Janey knew that Adam had

worked with lots of dogs, but she was impressed by how quickly he taught Truman the commands for sit, stay, come, and heel.

Truman seemed to enjoy all the attention. After a few days, Kitty reported that he was already acting friendlier with people—even ones he didn't know.

"He's a fast learner," she said as she watched Truman follow Janey around the lobby on Friday afternoon, staying right at her heel. "And you kids are great teachers! I bet he'll find his new family before long."

"I sure hope you're right. Sit, Truman!" Janey beamed as the little dog lowered his haunches to the floor. "Good boy!"

9

A Perfect Pair?

"I wish we didn't have to take him back to the shelter," Janey said as she turned the corner onto Third Street. It was early Sunday afternoon and she, Lolli, and Adam had just helped Kitty take Truman to the town park for a walk. The little dog had behaved perfectly, walking politely on his leash, letting several strangers pet him, and even standing quietly while a woman pushed a screaming baby past in a stroller.

"We shouldn't keep him out too long, though," Adam pointed out. "Lots of people come to the shelter on Sundays."

"That's right." Kitty gave a gentle tug on Truman's leash as he stopped to sniff at a leaf on the sidewalk. "We don't want him to miss being seen by his perfect adopter."

"True." Janey felt a pang of sadness. Even though they were all working hard to make Truman more adoptable, she hated to think that she might not get to see him anymore once he went to his new home.

When they entered the lobby, Truman barked and leaped forward. Zach and his mother were by the desk with one of Kitty's coworkers. Zach was balanced on one foot on his skateboard while Dr. Goldman examined a fat white cat's paw.

"Hi, Truman!" Zach exclaimed, hurrying forward to greet the little dog. "What's up?"

"We just went for a walk." Janey took Truman's leash from Kitty, and pulled him in closer. "Truman did fab. We're still working on his training, you know."

"Yeah, I heard." Zach rubbed Truman's head. "I bet someone will adopt him soon."

Janey nodded, stepping out of the way as the other shelter worker walked past carrying the white cat. "I'm thinking of posting again on my blog about how great Truman is doing," Janey said. "I bet that will get more people to come see him."

The bell over the shelter door tinkled as someone entered. Janey was surprised to see that it was Ms. Tanaka.

"Hi, kids!" The teacher seemed surprised to see them, too. She smiled. "You sure spend a lot of time here, don't you?"

"What can I say?" Zach shrugged and hooked a thumb toward his mother. "My mom drags me here all the time."

"I think she was talking to us," Janey informed him. "Hi, Ms. T. Didn't you already pick out a dog last weekend?" She'd been so busy thinking about Truman that she'd almost forgotten about her teacher's quest for a pet. But now she was curious.

"Not yet." The teacher shrugged. "There are lots of great dogs here, but I couldn't decide on one, so I decided to wait and think about it."

"So you came back for another look?" Kitty asked cheerfully. "I can help you as soon as I finish showing Dr. Goldman her next patient, okay?"

"No hurry, thanks." Ms. Tanaka smiled as Kitty and Dr. Goldman headed off into the dog room. Then she patted Truman as he trotted over to say hi. "Who have we here?"

"This is Truman—the dog we showed you before," Lolli told her.

Ms. Tanaka looked surprised. "Really? Wow, I didn't recognize him! He looks totally different from that poor, scraggly dog in the picture." She rubbed his ears, smiling as he slurped her hands and then rolled onto his back, begging for a belly rub. "Too bad he's not a little bigger."

Janey shot Lolli and Adam a look. Ms. Tanaka really seemed to like Truman—and he seemed to like her, too. Maybe they'd given up on her too easily!

"He might not be that big, but he's got a huge personality," Janey told Ms. Tanaka. "He's just about fully trained, too—watch!" She snapped her fingers to get Truman's attention. "Truman, heel!"

She quickly put Truman through his paces, demonstrating all the commands he could do. Truman got a little distracted when a shelter worker led a tiny, fluffy dog past, heading for the Meet and Greet room. But otherwise he was practically perfect!

When the demonstration was finished, Ms. Tanaka was smiling. "Very impressive,

Janey," she said. "Truman is cute. He'll make someone a fantastic friend. I'm just not sure he's quite what I'm looking for."

"Are you sure?" Janey's heart sank. What more could they do to convince her?

Zach stepped forward. "Can I take him for a sec?" he asked, reaching for Truman's leash.

Janey almost didn't hand him the leash. This was no time for Zach to start goofing around! She was sure if she could just figure out how to change Ms. Tanaka's mind somehow…

But she didn't resist as Zach took the leash. "Okay, Janey already showed you the boring stuff," he told Ms. Tanaka with a grin. "Now watch this!"

"What's he doing?" Lolli murmured, leaning toward Janey.

Janey shrugged. She watched as Zach kneeled down in front of Truman.

"Okay, Truman," he said, lifting his hand. "High-five!"

Truman barked. Then he jumped up, smacking his front paws onto Zach's palm.

"Oh, that's cute!" Ms. Tanaka exclaimed with a laugh. "Did you really teach him to high-five, Zach?"

"That's nothing," Zach said. "Check this out." He grabbed his skateboard and set it in front of Truman.

"Who taught Truman to high-five?" Lolli sounded confused.

Janey knew how she felt. She watched as

Truman jumped onto Zach's skateboard and then used his hind leg to push off, barking happily as he rode the skateboard halfway across the lobby.

This time Ms. Tanaka laughed out loud and clapped. "That's so cool!" she exclaimed. "Did you teach him that, Zach? Very impressive!"

Zach grinned and bowed. "Thank you, it was nothing," he said. "I've been coming by and teaching Truman a few tricks while Mom's here working."

Janey frowned, not sure whether to be impressed or annoyed. Then she noticed that Ms. Tanaka was kneeling down and patting Truman, whose whole body seemed to be wagging as he enjoyed the attention.

"Truman is great, isn't he?" Janey told her teacher. And then she had an idea. "He's kind of like a big dog in a little dog's body, right?"

"Yeah," Adam put in. "I've worked with a lot of dogs, and Truman is one of the coolest. Seriously."

Lolli nodded vigorously. "And I think he really likes you, Ms. Tanaka."

The teacher laughed, holding up her hands. "Okay, enough with the hard sell, gang," she said. "You don't need to convince me—Truman already did that."

"What? Really?" Janey wasn't sure she'd heard her right.

"Really." Ms. Tanaka gave Truman one last pat, then straightened up. "Actually, I've been thinking my apartment might be kind of small for a big dog. And now I'm totally convinced. Besides, a bigger dog couldn't ride a skateboard like that, right?" She winked. "Anyway, when Kitty comes back I think I'll talk to her about taking Truman home with me so I can see what other fun tricks I can teach him. What do you say, Truman?"

Truman barked and danced around her legs. Janey let out a whoop of joy. Talk about a happy ending!

10

Happy Endings… and Beginnings

"Leave that alone, Roscoe." Lolli tugged on her dog's leash as he stopped to sniff at a pinecone on the sidewalk. "Come on, we're almost there."

Janey stopped to let them catch up. It was Tuesday afternoon, and she and Lolli had decided to take Roscoe to the town park.

"Hey, look who's here!" Lolli said as they entered the park. "It's Ms. Tanaka and Truman!"

Janey looked where she was pointing. Their teacher was halfway across the park in a grassy area shaded by some huge old oak trees. Truman was there, too, chasing a ball his new owner was throwing for him.

"I still can't believe how great everything turned out." Lolli smiled as she watched the pair playing. "It's like it was meant to be!"

"I know, right?" Janey nodded. "Ms. Tanaka told me she can't imagine her life without Truman. Isn't that fab?"

"Totally fab," Lolli agreed. "Should we go over and say hi?"

Before she could answer, Janey heard a flurry of barking from the opposite direction. Turning to look, she saw Adam coming with one of his doggy clients, a pretty collie mix. Zach was with him, pushing himself along on his skateboard.

Roscoe's whole hind end wagged along with his tail as he greeted the other dog. The collie mix barked, then came forward to sniff Roscoe's nose.

"It's okay," Adam told Lolli. "This guy is friendly with other dogs. And I know Roscoe is, too."

Zach was peering across the park. "Hey, there's Ms. T and Truman," he said.

"Yeah, we just saw them, too," Janey said. "We were about to go say hi. Want to come?"

"In a minute." Adam glanced at Zach. "Actually, it's good that we ran into you. Zach has an idea he wants to tell you about."

"An idea?" Janey looked at Zach. "What kind of idea?"

Zach flipped his skateboard and tried to jump back on, but he missed and staggered off a few steps. "It's an idea about breaking my leg," he joked. "I'm working on it now."

Adam smiled. "No, seriously, tell them, dude," he said. "I think they'll like it."

"What is it, Zach?" Lolli asked.

Zach patted Roscoe as the big dog came over to sniff at him. "It's no big deal," he said. "Just something I was thinking about, you know? After what happened with Truman, and everything...."

Janey sighed. "Just spit it out already," she said. "We don't have all day."

Zach smirked. "Why not? Do you have an appointment with the President of the United States or something?"

"Just tell them," Adam said.

Zach shrugged. "Okay. See, we did such a great job getting Truman the perfect home, right? All of us helped."

"That's true," Lolli agreed.

Janey nodded. She had to admit that Zach's tricks had probably won over Ms. Tanaka just as much as the training she, Lolli, and Adam had done.

"So." Zach paused, glancing over toward Truman again. "I was thinking we should, you know, do more of that."

"You mean we should volunteer at the shelter?" Janey said. "We're already planning to."

"Not just that," Adam said. "He thinks we should form, like, a club or something."

"Yeah." Zach sounded excited now. "I was thinking we could call it the Pet Rescue Club! I bet there are lots of other animals right here in our town who need

114

our help. We could use your blog to find them, and then to help find them homes—just like with Truman. And, well, like I said, the four of us make a pretty good team…"

Lolli smiled. "What a super idea!" she exclaimed.

But, Janey hesitated. She wasn't so sure. For one thing, Zach was pretty annoying sometimes. Did she really want to be in a club with him?

"What do you think, Janey?" Adam asked.

"I don't know," Janey said slowly. "My blog is supposed to be for sharing cute pet photos, not for stuff like that. Seeing that first picture of Truman pop up was really upsetting."

"I know, but it could be for both things, couldn't it?" Lolli said, stroking the collie mix's sleek head. "We'll be able to help other dogs like Truman. And cats and other animals, too, of course."

"Isn't that worth being upset a little bit?" Adam added.

Zach didn't say anything. He was watching Janey carefully, not cracking jokes or messing with his skateboard for once. Janey stared back at him. Would he really take something like this seriously?

She wasn't sure, but she realized something else. It didn't matter. She took helping animals seriously. So did Lolli and Adam, and probably Zach. Working together, she was sure they could make it work.

"I guess you're right," she said with a cautious smile. "Helping Truman made it all worthwhile. And my blog has been getting tons of hits. Everyone loved hearing about Truman's happy ending. It really is the perfect way to reach animals in need."

"Cool!" Zach exclaimed with a grin. "So we're going to do this?"

He raised his hand. Lolli high-fived him. Adam switched the leash he was holding to his other hand and did the same. Then Janey stepped forward and high-fived Zach, too. At least she tried to—at the last second, he pulled his hand away.

"Psych!" he cried with a grin.

Janey frowned. "Very funny."

"Sorry." Zach grabbed her hand and

high-fived it. "So it's official—we're the Pet Rescue Club?"

"Yeah." Janey's mind was already filling with ideas for how to make the club work. It was going to be great! She couldn't believe she hadn't thought of it herself. "It's official. I can't wait to get started!"

Kids Getting Involved

Are you a kid who loves animals and wants to help them? Then get involved! Some shelters, like the one in Janey's town, allow kids to volunteer. Depending on the shelter you might be able to walk dogs, clean cages, feed the animals, talk to potential adopters about the pets that are waiting for their forever homes, play with the cats and dogs, and more.

For safety reasons, many shelters will only let adults volunteer.

If the shelter in your town has that rule, there are still lots of ways you can help their animals. Here are just a few ideas.

1. Organize a fundraiser for your local shelter or rescue. See if your school will let you have a bake sale. Maybe you can set up a lemonade stand by your house, or even have a yard sale if your parents say it is okay. Then you can donate all the money you make to the shelter.

2. Organize a drive to collect food and/or toys for shelter pets.

3. Read your shelter's website and other animal welfare sites to keep up on current needs and issues, and to learn about other ways to help.

4. Set an example for all pet owners by always treating your own pet well!

For more ideas, check out: *www.aspca.org/ parents/term/how-your-kids-can-help-shelter-pets*

Almost all shelter animals benefit from people just spending time with them. It helps make them feel calm and safe and relaxed. And that, in turn, can help them present themselves better when potential adopters come by. One great way to spend time with shelter pets is to read to them. Most pets find the sound of a voice reading aloud very soothing. If your local shelter will let you, why not take this book and read it to the cats and dogs there?

Meet the
Real Truman!

A little gray dog named Harry Truman was surrendered to a shelter in Tennessee in 2010. He was skinny and had matted fur. He was sent to a shelter in upstate New York, where he met his future owner. She considered herself a "big dog" person, but Harry Truman convinced her that even little dogs have big hearts!

No Time for Hallie

by Catherine Hapka
illustrated by Dana Regan

1
Bird Alert

"Good kitty, Mulberry." Janey Whitfield patted the fat orange tabby cat that had just jumped onto the sofa beside her. She giggled as he rubbed his face on her arm. "Your whiskers tickle! Aw, but that's okay— you love me, don't you?"

"He's just hoping you'll give him more food," Zach Goldman said with a laugh.

Mulberry was Zach's family's cat. Janey was at Zach's house, along with their friends Lolli Simpson and Adam Santos. Today was the first official meeting of the Pet Rescue Club—the group the four of them had decided to form after helping to rescue a neglected dog.

The meeting had started half an hour earlier. Zach's dad had brought out some snacks, and the four kids were supposed to be discussing how to organize their new group. But, they'd been too busy eating and playing with Mulberry to do much discussing so far.

Lolli selected a piece of cheese off the tray on the coffee table. "Did you add the stuff about the Pet Rescue Club to the blog?" she asked Janey.

"Yes." Janey pushed Mulberry away gently. Then she picked up her tablet computer and showed Lolli the screen.

Janey's blog had started as a way for kids around their town to share photos of their pets. Janey loved animals, but she couldn't have a pet of her own because her father was severely allergic to anything with fur or feathers. She'd thought that seeing pictures of lots of cute pets would be the next best thing to having her own.

Now the blog had another purpose, too. The Pet Rescue Club was going to use it to find animals that needed their help. So far Janey had written an update on the rescued dog and added a paragraph telling people to send in information on any animal that might need their help.

"Okay," Adam said. "So we put something on the blog. Now what?"

Adam was a very practical person. He was so responsible that he already had a successful pet-sitting business, even though he was only nine. People all over town paid him to come to their houses to feed and walk their dogs while they were at work or on vacation.

Janey didn't answer Adam right away. Mulberry was kneading his front paws on her leg and purring. Janey rubbed the cat's head and smiled.

"I wish I could have a cat like Mulberry," she said.

"Yeah, Mulberry is great!" Lolli leaned over to pet the cat. Mulberry turned around and butted his head against her arm.

Janey giggled. "And he's so cute! Here, Mulberry—want a cracker?"

"Don't give him that," Zach said quickly. "It's onion flavored and cats shouldn't eat onion—it's bad for them."

"Really?" Janey wasn't sure whether to believe him. Zach was always joking around and playing pranks on people. Still, she didn't want to hurt Mulberry if Zach was being serious for once. She pulled the cracker away and glanced at Adam. "Is that true? Are onions bad for cats?"

Adam shrugged. "Probably. I know dogs aren't supposed to eat onions."

"Why are you asking him? Don't you believe me?" Zach asked Janey. "My mom's a vet, you know. She's taught me lots of stuff like that."

Before Janey could answer, a pair of twelve-year-old boys raced into the room.

They were identical twins. Both of them were tall and skinny with wavy dark hair and the same brown eyes as Zach. It was raining outside, and the boys' sneakers left wet tracks on the floor.

Janey knew the twins were two of Zach's three older brothers. She couldn't imagine living with that many boys!

"Check it out," one of the twins said, pointing at Janey. "Little Zachie has a girlfriend!"

"No way—he has two girlfriends! Way to go, little bro!" the other boy exclaimed with a grin.

"Shut up!" Zach scowled at them. "And go away. We're trying to have a meeting here."

One of the twins stepped over and grabbed Mulberry off the sofa. "Yo, Mulberry," he said, cuddling the cat. "Are these girls bothering you?"

"Mulberry likes us," Lolli said with a

smile. "He's like the mascot of the Pet Rescue Club."

"Okay." The twin dropped Mulberry on the sofa again. The cat sat down and started washing his paw.

"Grab the umbrella and let's go," the other twin said. "The guys are waiting for us outside."

One of the twins grabbed an umbrella off a hook by the back door. Then they raced back out of the room.

"Sorry about that," Zach muttered. "They are so annoying."

"They're not so bad." Lolli smiled. She got along with everybody—even obnoxious boys. "Anyway, what were we talking about?"

"About how cats can't eat onion," Zach

said. "They shouldn't have chocolate, either. Did you know that?" He stared at Janey.

She shrugged. "No. That's interesting."

"Yeah," Lolli agreed. "There's lots to know about having a pet! When we first got Roscoe, I thought all he needed was a bowl of water and some dog food. But there's a lot more to it than that!"

Roscoe was the Simpsons' big, lovable dog. Lolli and her parents had found him at the Third Street Shelter a few years earlier. He was a mix of Labrador retriever, rottweiler, and who knew what else.

"I have an idea," Janey said. "You already said Mulberry was our club mascot. We should make Roscoe a mascot, too. We can post their pictures on the blog to make it official."

"Good idea," Lolli said. "I have a cute picture of Roscoe we can use."

"We should take a picture of Mulberry riding on my skateboard," Zach said. "That would be cool!"

"Veto," Janey replied.

Zach frowned at her. "Can't you just say no like a normal person?" he said. "Oh, wait, I forgot—you're not normal."

Janey ignored him. "Veto" was her new favorite word. Janey liked finding interesting words and using them. Saying veto was her new way of saying no.

"Hey Janey," Adam spoke up. "I think I heard your tablet ping."

"Really?" Janey had dropped her tablet

on the sofa. Now Mulberry was sitting on it. She pulled the tablet out from under the cat. "Sorry, Mulberry. That might be an animal who needs our help!"

Lolli leaned over her shoulder. "What does it say?"

"It's not a posting on the blog," Janey said. "It's alerting me to a new e-mail."

She clicked into her e-mail account. The message was from a classmate named Leah. Janey read it quickly.

Hi Janey,

I heard you're helping animals now. I need help! I just got home from my soccer practice and found out my pet canary is missing!

2
Runaway Cat?

"Oh, no!" Janey exclaimed, reading the e-mail again.

"What's wrong?" Adam asked.

"The e-mail is from Leah," Janey said. "She says her canary is missing!"

"Leah has a canary?" Lolli said. "I didn't know that."

"I didn't either. But if it's missing, we should try to help her find it," Janey said. "Zach, can I use the phone?"

"Sure, that'll be five dollars, please," Zach said.

Janey ignored the joke. She rushed into

the kitchen and grabbed the phone. Leah had put her number at the end of the e-mail.

"Janey?" Leah said from the other end of the line. "I was hoping you'd call. I'm so worried about Sunny!"

"What happened?" Janey asked.

"I must have forgotten to latch his cage after I fed him this morning before school." Leah sounded upset. "When I got home, the cage door was open and Sunny was nowhere in sight!"

"Oh, no," Janey exclaimed.

"That's not even the worst part," Leah went on. "My bedroom window was open! What if he flew outside? I might never find him!"

Janey glanced at Lolli, Adam, and Zach. They had followed her into the kitchen and were all listening to her half of the conversation.

"Don't worry, Leah," Janey said. "The Pet Rescue Club is on it! We'll be right over."

She hung up and told the others what Leah had said. "I don't like the idea of keeping birds cooped up in cages," Lolli said uncertainly. "Shouldn't they be free to fly around?"

"I don't know," Janey said. "But Leah sounded really worried."

"Then we should help her," Lolli said.

"Definitely," Zach agreed, and Adam nodded.

Mulberry had followed Janey into the kitchen, too. He rubbed against her legs. Then, suddenly, he meowed and rushed over to the screen door leading outside.

"Mulberry, what are you doing?" Lolli asked.

"Look!" Adam pointed. "There's another cat out there!"

Janey saw it, too. A cute black cat with big green eyes was looking in at them from outside!

"Where did that cat come from?" Lolli wondered.

"I don't know." Janey stepped closer and peered at the cat. "It's not wearing a collar or tags. But it looks healthy—just wet from the rain."

"I think I know where that cat lives," Zach said. "I've seen her in the window of a house across the street."

Lolli looked concerned. "Uh-oh. What if she slipped out when her owners weren't looking? They'll be worried sick."

Adam nodded. "We should take her home."

"Yeah." Zach grinned. "This is the perfect chance for the Pet Rescue Club to rescue another pet!"

Janey felt impatient. "Okay, but hurry," she said. "Leah is waiting, remember?"

Zach ran to tell his father where they were going. Then the kids all went outside. Zach had to nudge Mulberry away from the door to stop him from following them.

The black cat was just as friendly as Mulberry. She rubbed against Lolli's legs and purred.

"Good kitty," Lolli said. "Can I pick you up?"

The cat purred louder. "I think she's saying yes," Janey said with a smile.

Lolli picked up the cat. "Which house is it?" she asked, squinting in the light rain.

"That one." Zach pointed to a white house with black shutters. "My parents have met the people who live here, but I don't know them at all. They only moved in last summer."

All four kids checked for traffic and then crossed the street. The cat stayed snuggled in Lolli's arms.

Janey led the way up the steps onto the front porch of the white house. There was no doorbell, but there was a brass knocker shaped like a seashell. Janey reached up and rapped the knocker two or three times.

They waited but there was no response. "Maybe they're not home," Adam said.

"Try knocking one more time," Lolli suggested.

"Here, let me do it. Janey knocks like

a girl." Zach pushed past the others and knocked harder. "There. If they're home, they should hear that."

Janey rolled her eyes at Lolli. Lolli just smiled.

Finally, there was the sound of footsteps from inside. Then the door swung open. A young woman was standing there. She was wearing sweatpants, and her hair was in a messy ponytail. A chubby baby with rosy cheeks was balanced on one hip.

"Oh, hello, kids," the woman said. "What are you doing with Hall Cat?"

"Hall Cat?" Lolli giggled. "Is that really her name?"

The young woman smiled back, though

she didn't look that happy. "Yes, that's her," she said. "Was she bothering you? Sometimes she's too friendly for her own good."

"No, she wasn't bothering us," Janey said. "We thought you might be looking for her, though. We found her outside." She smiled at the baby. He was staring at her with big, blue eyes.

"Yes, my husband let her out a little while ago." The young woman shifted the baby to her other hip. "Hall Cat is sweet, but ever since the baby came, she always seems to be underfoot." She wiped a spot of drool off the baby's chin. "I'm afraid I might trip over her and drop him."

"Oh." Janey looked at Hall Cat. The cat was still purring away in Lolli's arms, looking content and calm. "Um, maybe you didn't know, but being outside can be dangerous for a house cat. She could get hit by a car, or—"

"This is a quiet neighborhood," the young mother broke in. "Anyway, we had

to do something. What if she scratched the
baby while she was trying to play with him?
I can't take that chance."

She sounded so worried that Janey
couldn't help feeling sorry for her. But Janey

was worried about Hall Cat, too.

"Maybe you could keep the baby's door shut," she said. "Or—"

Just then the baby let out a loud gurgle. The young woman glanced at him.

"Thanks for being so concerned about Hall Cat, kids," she said. "But trust me, being outside is the best option we have right now. My husband and I don't want to take her to the shelter, so she'll just have to adjust."

"The shelter?" Zach sounded alarmed.

"But—" Janey began.

Suddenly the baby opened his mouth and started to wail. His mother winced, then hugged him to her, rocking him back and forth.

"Sorry, I really have to go," she said. "You can leave Hall Cat on the porch if you want—she seems to like it there. Bye now!"

Before Janey could come up with another way to change the woman's mind, the door swung shut.

3

Search and Rescue

"I still don't think we should have left Hall Cat outside," Zach said. It was a few minutes later, and the Pet Rescue Club was halfway to Leah's house. She only lived a few blocks away in the same neighborhood.

"I know." Janey shrugged. "But what else could we do? Break into her owners' house and sneak her back in?"

"We're supposed to be the Pet Rescue Club." Lolli kicked at a stone on the sidewalk. "We should try to figure out how to help Hall Cat."

"We will," Janey said. "Right after we help Leah find her bird."

She felt sorry for Hall Cat, too. But she was even more worried about Leah's canary.

Soon the Pet Rescue Club was ringing Leah's doorbell. Leah answered right away. She was a tall, skinny girl with freckles and glasses. Normally she was always smiling or laughing, but today she looked anxious and sad.

"Thanks for coming," she said. "Come in and I'll show you Sunny's cage."

Janey and the others went inside. Leah's four-year-old brother was sitting on the living room floor playing with a toy car. Two cats were watching him. One was a gray tabby, and the other was mostly white with brown and orange patches.

"Cute kitties," Lolli told Leah.

"Thanks." Leah barely glanced at the cats as she headed for the stairs. Janey guessed that she was too worried about Sunny to think about anything else.

The Pet Rescue Club followed Leah to her bedroom upstairs. The room was painted pale yellow with white trim. Along one wall was a bird cage. It was very tall, with several perches, a mirror, and colorful hanging toys.

"Wow." Lolli sounded impressed as she stepped closer for a better look. "This is a really nice cage!"

"Thanks," Leah said with a sad sigh. "Sunny loves it—at least I thought he did."

"It's so big," Zach commented. "Is it really all for one little bird?"

"Yes." Leah touched the cage. "Canaries need lots of room to fly. That's why Sunny's cage is so big."

"Really? That's interesting." Janey read everything she could about animals. But she didn't know that much about pet birds. "So you don't have any other canaries to keep Sunny company? Do you think that's why he flew away?"

Lolli nodded. "That makes sense. Maybe he was looking for a friend."

"Dogs like having other dogs around," Adam agreed.

"Actually, male canaries do better living alone," Leah said. "And like I said, Sunny seemed really happy. I don't know why he'd try to escape!"

"We should try to find him." Adam walked over to the window and looked out. "Maybe he's still in your backyard."

All five of them hurried downstairs and out the back door. For the next half hour, they searched Leah's backyard. The yard was pretty big, and had lots of shrubs and flowers. Janey didn't like getting her hands dirty, but she was willing to do it to help an animal. She pulled back the branches of a prickly rose bush, looking for a flash of yellow. But there was no sign of Sunny.

"Here, birdie, birdie!" Zach called. He whistled loudly.

"Not like that," Leah corrected. "He likes it when I whistle to him like this."

She let out a soft, musical whistle. Janey tried to imitate it, and couldn't do it. But Adam imitated the whistle perfectly!

"Dude!" Zach said with a laugh. "You sound like a canary! I always knew you were a birdbrain!"

"Quit joking around," Janey told him. "We need to find Sunny before it gets dark."

"I know." Zach shot a look at Leah. "Sorry. I'll look over there behind the shed."

Another twenty minutes passed with no sign of Sunny. Finally, the back door opened and Leah's mom looked out.

"Leah, are you out there?" she called.

"Sorry, but it's time for your friends to go home now. You need to set the table for dinner."

"But we haven't found Sunny yet!" Leah sounded frantic.

"I'm sorry, honey." Her mother did sound sorry, but she also sounded firm. "Maybe Sunny will find his way home on his own. There's nothing else you can do right now."

Leah sighed as her mother disappeared. "I'm so worried," she told Janey and the others, her voice quavering. "Poor little Sunny! He's not used to being out on his own."

"I know." Janey put an arm around her shoulders. "Try not to worry. The Pet Rescue Club will figure something out. I promise."

Zach hated waking up early. He always felt sleepy until almost lunchtime.

But the next morning when he looked out his bedroom window, he felt wide-awake right away. A small black shape was sitting on the sidewalk in front of his house.

"Hall Cat," Zach murmured. He tapped on the glass, but Hall Cat didn't hear him. She was watching a bird pecking at the grass nearby.

Moments later, Zach was dressed and heading for the door. He almost tripped over Mulberry, who was sleeping on the kitchen floor.

"Where are you going, dork?" his oldest brother, Josh, called out.

"Back in a sec," Zach said without slowing down.

Hall Cat came running when she saw Zach. She purred as he picked her up. Her fur felt soft and warm.

"Good girl," Zach whispered, tickling her chin. "I'm going to take you home, okay?"

Hall Cat kept purring. Zach carried her across the street. Even before he knocked on the door, he could hear the baby crying inside. A young man with a goatee answered Zach's knock.

"Hi," Zach said. "I found your cat outside."

The man peered at him. "You're one of the boys from across the street, right?" he said. "Hi there. Oh, and don't worry about Hall Cat. She likes it outside."

"Maybe," Zach said. "But it's dangerous out there. Um, you know, cars and stuff." He tried to remember what else he'd heard Janey and the others say.

"No, it's cool, seriously." The man said smiling, but he looked distracted. "We've been putting her out whenever the baby's awake, and she's been fine."

Zach squeezed Hall Cat a little tighter, making her wiggle. He didn't want the man to close the door and leave Hall Cat outside. But Zach wasn't sure what to say to stop him. He wished Janey was there—she always had lots of things to say. Or Adam, who knew so much about taking care of animals. Or Lolli—people seemed to like talking to her, even grownups.

"Um, how long have you had Hall Cat?" Zach blurted out.

The man glanced over his shoulder as another loud wail came from somewhere inside. "Quite a while," he said. He chuckled. "Longer than I've had my wife, actually."

"Really?" Zach said.

The man reached out to scratch Hall Cat under the chin, which made her purr even louder. "I got her in college actually," he said.

"I was living in a fraternity house and found her huddled under the front porch. She was super-friendly, but none of our neighbors knew where she came from. So we kept her." He smiled. "She sort of became our fraternity mascot and visited everyone who lived on my hall. That's why we called her Hall Cat. After I graduated she stayed with me and the name had stuck."

"That's pretty funny," Zach said with a grin.

The man grinned back. "Anyway, when I got married a few years later, Hall Cat came to live with us. My wife had never had a pet before, but she's always liked Hall Cat." He sighed and glanced over his shoulder again as the baby let out a loud squawk somewhere inside. "But now, with the new baby, she's just a little overwhelmed and worried about what might happen, you know?"

Zach didn't really know what the man meant by that. Before he could ask, he heard a loud wheezing and clanking sound from the far end of the block.

"Oops," he said. "That's the school bus. Gotta go!"

He leaned to one side, tossing Hall Cat

gently past the man into the house. "Hey!" the man exclaimed, sounding surprised.

But Zach didn't stick around to find out whether the man threw Hall Cat back out or let her stay in. His backpack was still at home, and he'd have to run if he wanted to grab it before the bus got there.

4

Questions and Answers

When Janey got to school, she headed to Leah's cubby before even visiting her own. Leah was there putting her books away.

"Did you find him?" Janey asked.

As soon as Leah turned around, Janey could guess the answer. Leah still looked sad and worried.

"No," Leah said with a loud sigh. "I got up early this morning to search in the yard some more, but all I saw out there were wild birds and a few squirrels."

"Oh." Janey chewed her lower lip. "Okay, try not to worry. I'll figure something out, I promise."

She found Lolli at her cubby, which was right next to Janey's. Janey told her friend what she'd just found out from Leah.

"That's too bad," Lolli said. "Leah must be so worried."

"She is. And so am I." Janey noticed that Lolli didn't seem to be listening very carefully. She was looking at something over Janey's shoulder. When Janey looked that way, all she saw was one of their classmates, a girl named Brooke.

"Have you noticed that Brooke doesn't seem like her normal self?" Lolli whispered.

"Not really," Janey said. "What do you mean?"

"She's usually so happy and outgoing. But lately she's been a lot quieter. Today it even looks like she's been crying!" Lolli took a step toward Brooke. "I think I'll go ask her if anything's wrong."

"Wait!" Janey said. "We need to figure out what to do about Sunny."

It was too late. Lolli didn't hear her, because she was already hurrying toward Brooke. Letting out a sigh, Janey followed.

"Hi, Brooke," Lolli said when she reached the other girl. "Are you okay?"

Brooke was short with long, black hair. Right now her hair was hanging over her face, hiding one of her brown eyes. But the eye Janey could see looked sad.

"I'm fine," Brooke said.

"Are you sure?" Lolli put a hand on Brooke's arm. "You seem kind of upset or something. If you need someone to talk to…"

"No, really, I'm fine." Brooke said again. "I have to go."

Grabbing one more book out of her cubby, she rushed off. Lolli and Janey stared after her.

"She's definitely not fine," Lolli said. "Should we follow her and try to talk to her again?"

"Veto," Janey said. "We're supposed to be helping pets, not people, remember?"

Just then Zach zoomed up to the girls on his skateboard. "Hi," he greeted them breathlessly.

"You're not supposed to ride your skate-board in the halls," Janey reminded him. "Don't let the teachers see you, or you'll have to stay after school. And we'll probably need everyone in the Pet Rescue Club to help search for Leah's canary again today."

"Never mind that bird," Zach said. "We need to help Hall Cat. I found her outside again this morning."

He told Janey and Lolli what the neighbor had said. Lolli shook her head.

"I was hoping they'd let her come back inside after we talked to the baby's mom yesterday," she said. "I guess not."

"We need to convince them to take better care of Hall Cat," Zach said. "Or else she might get hit by a car or something!"

"I'm sure her owners don't want that,"

Lolli said. "They seem nice. Just kind of busy with the new baby."

Janey nodded. "Okay, we should definitely figure out a way to help Hall Cat," she said. "But what about Sunny? If a cat is in danger outside, what about a tiny little bird? I think we need to find him first, then come up with a plan for Hall Cat."

"No way," Zach said. "Hall Cat needs us right now!"

"Wow," Lolli said. "Now that we started the Pet Rescue Club, there are even more pets to help than I expected! I guess we need to figure out how to help two pets at once."

"Hall Cat will be fine for a few days," Janey argued. "There really isn't much traffic in our neighborhood."

"What if she wanders off and gets lost, though?" Zach argued back. "Or gets attacked by a mean dog, or eats something she shouldn't? There are some plants and stuff that are poisonous to cats—not just onions, either."

Before Janey could respond, she saw Adam walking toward them with Ms. Tanaka, their homeroom teacher. Ms. Tanaka was young and friendly and smiled a lot, which made her almost everyone's favorite teacher.

"Hi!" Janey called. "How's Truman?"

Truman was the dog that had inspired Janey and the others to start the Pet Rescue Club. With the help of the local animal shelter, the kids had worked together to save him from a neglectful home and help him find a new home with Ms. Tanaka.

"Truman is great!" Ms. Tanaka said with a smile. "I took him for a nice, long walk after school yesterday."

"That's awesome," Janey said. Hearing how well Truman was doing made her more determined than ever to help more animals—starting with Sunny.

Ms. Tanaka waved and headed into her classroom. After she was gone, Janey and the others told Adam what they'd been talking about.

"Okay, it sounds like we have two pets who need our help right away," Adam said. "Maybe we should divide and conquer."

"What do you mean?" Janey asked.

Adam shrugged. "There are four of us," he pointed out. "Maybe Zach should talk to Hall Cat's owners after school, and Janey and Lolli can go look for the lost bird."

"What about you?" Lolli asked.

"I'll come help whoever needs me after I take care of my clients," Adam said.

Janey thought about Adam's idea. It made sense. Zach was too hyper to be much help searching for Sunny, anyway.

"Wait, so I have to go talk to Hall Cat's owners all by myself?" Zach asked. "I was hoping you guys could help me convince them."

"Adam can come help you later," Janey said. "I think his plan could work. Let's do it!"

5
Kitty and Cats

Lolli usually liked school. But that day, she was happy when the final bell rang. She was worried about both of the pets that the Pet Rescue Club was trying to help. Besides, she'd had an idea she wanted to tell Janey and Leah about.

She walked out of the classroom with the two of them. "Ready to go to Leah's house and look for Sunny?" Janey asked her. "I already called my mom to come and drive us there so we don't have to wait for the bus."

"Actually, I was thinking about something," Lolli said. She turned to Leah. "Did you check with the Third Street Shelter after Sunny went missing? Maybe someone found him and took him there."

"I called them yesterday," Leah said. "Nobody had brought him in yet." She bit her lower lip. "Anyway, I doubt anyone except me could catch Sunny."

Janey nodded. "It's okay. He's probably still in your yard. We'll find him."

Janey sounded very certain. Lolli had heard her friend sound that way a lot. Sometimes it meant that Janey was so busy thinking about her own plans that she wasn't paying enough attention to what other people were saying. So Lolli cleared her throat and talked a little louder.

"Even if nobody could catch him, some-body might call the shelter to report seeing him," she said. "If you want, I'll call home and ask if it's okay for me to walk over there and check."

The animal shelter was only a few blocks from school. Lolli's parents had let her walk there before, so she guessed they would say yes today, too.

"That's a good idea," Leah said. "If some-one reported seeing Sunny, it will help us figure out if he's still in my backyard or if he flew somewhere else."

Janey blinked at Lolli. "Oh. Yeah, I guess that's true. Are you sure you don't mind going to the shelter by yourself?"

"It will be fine," Lolli said. "One of my parents can probably pick me up there and drive me over to meet you guys at Leah's house."

She said good-bye to Janey and Leah, then headed for the school office to call home. As she'd guessed, her father said it was okay to walk to the shelter. He promised to meet her there in a few minutes to pick her up.

As she walked down the sidewalk, Lolli spotted Brooke walking just ahead of her. Brooke's head was down, and her steps were slow.

"Hey, Brooke!" Lolli broke into a jog to catch up. "Wait up. Are you walking toward town, too?"

Brooke stopped and waited. "Uh-huh. I'm supposed to meet my dad at his office," she said. "Why are you walking this way? I thought you lived on a farm."

"I do." Lolli and the other girl both started walking again. "But today I'm going to the animal shelter." She told Brooke about the Pet Rescue Club and their search for Sunny.

"Wow," Brooke said. "That's cool that you guys are trying to help animals."

"Thanks." Lolli smiled at her. "Do you walk to your dad's office every day after school?"

"No, I usually take the bus." Brooke sighed. "But everything is different lately."

Lolli leaned closer. "What do you mean? Does it have to do with why you look so sad?" She reached over and gave Brooke's arm a squeeze. "Sorry, my parents tell me I'm too nosy. I just want to help if I can."

Brooke sniffled. Then she took a deep breath.

"You're nice, Lolli," she said. "I guess I can tell you. My grandpa fell and hurt himself a few weeks ago."

Lolli gasped. "Oh, no! Is he okay?"

"Not really." Brooke shrugged. "I mean, his broken hip is getting better, but he still can't walk by himself or go up and down the stairs. So instead of letting him go home after he got out of the hospital, they sent him to another place."

"Another place?" Lolli wrinkled her nose. "What do you mean?"

"It's called an assisted care facility," Brooke said. "He has to live there while he does lots of physical therapy and stuff. Nobody is sure how long that will take."

"Wow." Lolli thought about her own grandfathers. Her dad's dad sold real estate, and her mom's dad was retired but still played golf or tennis almost every day. "No wonder you're upset."

"Not as upset as my grandma." Brooke kicked a stone on the sidewalk. "She's living in their house all by herself now. She says she's fine, but I can tell she's sad and lonely without Grandpa around."

"Oh, that's terrible." Lolli's eyes filled with tears at the thought of Brooke's grandma being so sad.

Brooke nodded. "That's why I'm going to my dad's office. I'm planning to spend lots of time with Grandma to help her feel less lonely. Dad is going to drive me over there today."

"That's nice. I bet she'll love seeing you," Lolli said. "Let me know if I can do anything to help, okay? I'm good at reading to people if she might like that, or I can bake her some cookies…"

Brooke looked thoughtful. "Grandma can read to herself just fine," she said. "But actually, maybe there is something you can do…"

"Kitty?" Lolli stuck her head into the cat room at the Third Street Shelter. "The guy at the front desk said you were in here."

Kitty look up and smiled, spitting out a strand of blonde hair that was caught in her lip gloss. She was the Pet Rescue Club's favorite shelter worker.

"Hi, Lolli," Kitty said. "What brings you here today? I didn't see your name on the volunteer schedule." She winked. "Did you come to adopt another dog to keep Roscoe company?"

Lolli giggled. "I'd love to, but my parents would kill me." She stepped into the room to pet a cute tiger-striped cat that was wandering around while Kitty cleaned out her litter box. "Actually, I'm here on official Pet Rescue Club business."

She told Kitty about Sunny. By the time she was finished, Kitty was shaking her head.

"Sorry, no calls about a loose canary," she said. "I'll be sure to let you guys know right away if I hear anything, though."

"Thanks." Lolli leaned closer to the

cat, who had started purring as soon as Lolli started petting her. "Hey, I remember you from my first day volunteering here," Lolli cooed. "You're so cute! I can't believe nobody has adopted you yet."

Kitty nodded. "Yes, Tigs is adorable," she said. "But she's also ten years old, and unfortunately, most people don't want to take on a cat her age."

"Really?" Lolli couldn't help thinking about Hall Cat. Based on what her owner had told Zach, she was probably at least ten years old, too. "Why not?"

Kitty shrugged. "Older animals have a lot of love to give," she said. "But I guess it makes people sad to think they might not have an older pet for as long as a younger one. I don't know. But a cat of Tigs' age will be lucky if anyone even considers adopting her—no matter how cute and friendly she is."

Lolli nodded, feeling a flash of worry for Hall Cat. Her owners said they weren't planning to take her to the shelter. But what if they changed their minds?

They won't, she told herself firmly. I'm sure they'll decide to keep her—and keep her inside, too. After all, the Pet Rescue Club is on the case!

6
Different Strokes

"How many more clients do you have today?" Zach asked, feeling impatient. "I want to get to Hall Cat's house soon."

He'd decided to wait for Adam before starting his mission. Otherwise, he was afraid he wouldn't know what to say again. And that wouldn't help Hall Cat at all.

"Just one more," Adam said, pointing to a blue house up ahead. "It won't take long, since I just have to walk the dog and not feed it or anything."

"Really? Why, is the dog on a diet?" Zach grinned.

"Ha ha, very funny," Adam said. "It's because the owners just had twin babies."

"Twins?" Zach made a face. "I hope they're not anything like my obnoxious twin brothers."

Adam smiled. "Actually, these twins are pretty cute," he said. "But the mom has trouble walking the dog with both babies along, and the dad works all day in another town. So they hired me to walk the dog for them, at least until the twins are older."

"Oh." Zach thought about that. It reminded him of Hall Cat's owners, except they hadn't hired Adam to take care of their pet. They'd put her outside instead.

When Adam knocked on the door, a young woman with lots of dark curls and big brown eyes answered. Behind her, Zach could see a spacious living room. Two babies were playing with blocks on the rug. A large, fluffy collie was lying there watching them, but he jumped up and barked happily when he spotted Adam.

"Hi there, Brody." Adam rubbed the dog's ears as it rushed over to greet him. "Mrs. Cooper, this is my friend Zach Goldman. He's helping me today."

"Hi, Zach." Mrs. Cooper smiled as she handed Adam a leash. "Goldman—are you related to Brody's vet, Dr. Goldman?"

"Yeah, that's my mom," Zach said. He was used to having people ask about his mother. Almost all the pets in town went to her veterinary practice.

But he wasn't really thinking about his mom. He was still thinking about Hall Cat. He stared at Brody as Adam clipped the leash onto the dog's collar.

"Hey, Mrs. Cooper," Zach blurted out. "Did you think about making Brody live outside when you had your babies?"

Mrs. Cooper looked startled. Then she smiled and shook her head.

"No, not even for a second," she said, bending over to rub her dog's head. "Brody is part of the family. And in this family, that means living inside!"

"But isn't it a lot of work having a dog and twins?" Zach asked. "What if you trip over Brody or something?"

"I suppose it's a little extra work," Mrs. Cooper said, glancing over at the twins. "We had to make sure to introduce Brody to the babies slowly, and we always watch carefully when he's with them." She shrugged. "Any extra work is worth it, though."

"Come on, Zach," Adam said. "Brody is ready for his walk."

Zach kept thinking about what Mrs. Cooper had said as he wandered along after Adam and Brody. He was glad that Brody had such nice owners. But he was more worried than ever about Hall Cat. What could he and the rest of the Pet Rescue Club do to convince her owners to change their minds about keeping her outside?

~~~

"Do you think Sunny joined a flock of wild birds or something?" Janey asked, peering at a bird perched on a branch overhead.

She was in Leah's backyard. The two of them had been searching for Sunny all afternoon. First they'd looked in the back-yard. Then they'd checked the front yard, and then the empty lot across the street. Finally,

they'd returned to the backyard, since that was the closest to Leah's bedroom window.

"I doubt it," Leah said. "Male canaries are solitary. They like to have their own space."

"Really?" Janey pursed her lips. "Wait. Then why are you so sure he flew out the window?"

Leah shrugged. "I'm not sure. But I haven't heard him in the house since he disappeared. Or heard him singing, either."

"Okay," Janey said. "But if you were a tiny bird, and you were loose in a house with a couple of cats and a loud little kid, wouldn't you keep quiet?"

Leah's eyes widened. "You're right! I barely searched inside at all. I was so sure he flew out the window, I didn't even think about him being in the house."

Janey had been feeling discouraged. But now she was excited again. She might have just cracked the case of the missing canary!

"Come on, Leah." She headed for the back door. "Let's go search inside now!"

7

The Search Is On

Soon Janey and Leah were searching inside Leah's house. Leah's little brother was taking a nap, and her mother was busy on the computer in the den, so the house was quiet. After a while, the gray tabby cat noticed what the two girls were doing and started following them.

"Scat, Buddy," Leah told the cat. "Trust me, Sunny doesn't want to see you right now."

The cat ignored her, rubbing against Janey's legs. Normally Janey loved cats just as much as she loved all animals. But right now seeing one of Leah's cats made her feel uneasy. Cats liked to hunt smaller animals—including birds. What if Leah's cats decided to hunt Sunny?

"We need to find Sunny fast," she said.

Leah glanced at the cat. "I know. But how? If he's scared and hiding, we might never find him!"

Janey thought for a second. "I've got it," she said. "You told us that Sunny likes it when you whistle to him, right?"

"Right," Leah replied. "It makes him happy, and he usually starts singing." She gasped. "Janey, you're a genius! Maybe if I whistle, Sunny will answer!"

"What are you waiting for?" Janey smiled. She liked being called a genius! "Start whistling!"

They walked around the house slowly, with Leah whistling a merry tune the whole way. Janey listened as hard as she could. Would Sunny answer?

"There!" she cried as they passed an open doorway leading into a bedroom. "I heard something—a whistle!"

"It's Sunny!" Leah exclaimed. She stepped into the room and whistled. Once again, there was a whistle in return!

Janey looked down at Buddy. The cat was still following the girls. He'd stopped and sat down in the bedroom doorway. But he pricked up his ears toward the room and twitched his tail.

Leah stepped into the room and looked around. "I don't see him," she said. "He must be hiding."

There were lots of places to hide in the room. It seemed to be the place where Leah's family put everything that didn't have another place to go. There were a couple of bookshelves packed full of books and other stuff, a bed with tons of pillows, and lots of other odds and ends of furniture. Several cardboard boxes were stacked in one corner, and the half-open closet door barely contained all the clothes and other things inside. How were they ever going to find a tiny bird in there?

Once again, Janey started thinking hard. She looked around the room and spotted another door.

"Does that door open into your bedroom?" she asked Leah.

"Actually, it opens into the bathroom," Leah said. "I share it with this room—this is just a guest room, so the bathroom is mostly mine."

Janey nodded. Then she bent down and gently shoved Buddy into the hall. "Sorry, Buddy," she said as she shut the door in the cat's face. "But we don't need your help with this."

"What are you doing?" Leah asked. "Do you have an idea for how to get Sunny to come out? I'm still not sure he'll let me catch him, though." She looked worried. "He must be awfully scared if this is the first time he's sung in two days!"

"Don't worry, I have a plan." Janey hurried over and opened the door into the bathroom. She continued through the small room into Leah's bedroom. When she entered, Buddy was just strolling in from the hall. "Eh, eh, eh!" Janey scolded the cat gently. She scooped him up and deposited him back in the hallway. "Like I just told you, we don't need your help right now."

She closed the bedroom door, shutting the cat out. But she left the doors between the bathroom and the two bedrooms wide open.

"Okay," she said to Leah, who had followed her into her bedroom. "Now we need to put all of Sunny's favorite foods in his cage, and leave the door open. We'll sit very still, and you'll whistle to try to call him in."

Leah nodded. "I get it! We can lure him into his cage. It could work!"

They set Janey's plan into motion right away. Leah filled Sunny's food dishes with lots of tasty treats. Then she and Janey crouched down near the cage.

"Okay," Janey said. "Now, whistle!"

Leah took a deep breath and whistled her song. At first nothing happened. Janey started to feel worried. What if Sunny couldn't hear them from the other room?

She shifted her weight. Sitting still and being quiet weren't Janey's favorite things. But she knew that if she moved at the wrong time, she might scare Sunny. So she did her best to act like a statue.

"I don't know if this is going to work," Leah whispered. "I don't hear any—wait! There he is!"

Janey heard it, too. Sunny was singing again! And he sounded closer!

"Keep whistling," she whispered. "I think he's in the bathroom now!"

Leah nodded and whistled her song again. Sunny didn't answer this time. But a moment later Janey saw a flash of bright yellow zip in through the bathroom door. It was Sunny! The little canary flew over and perched on top of his cage.

Janey held her breath. Beside her, Leah stopped whistling. Janey could see that the other girl's fingers were crossed, and she guessed that they were both thinking the same thing. Would Sunny go back into his cage?

The next few minutes seemed to last about forty-two days, at least to Janey. But finally, Sunny hopped down onto the top of his cage door. He perched there for another few seconds, then flew right into the cage!

"Oh, Sunny!" Leah cried as she leaped up and snapped the door shut. "It's so good to have you home!"

The little bird pecked at his food. Then he let out a trill before going back to eating.

Janey grinned. "We did it!"

"You did it." Leah spun around and hugged her. "Thank you so much! I don't know what I would have done without you."

"It was nothing," Janey said modestly. "Just another successful case for the Pet Rescue Club."

8
Zach's Mission

"A toast to Janey!" Lolli cried, lifting her bottle of juice.

"And the Pet Rescue Club!" Adam added.

"And the Pet Rescue Club," Lolli agreed.

"Thanks, guys," Janey said with a smile. It was the next day at lunchtime. The four members of the Pet Rescue Club were sitting together in the school cafeteria. Actually, Janey, Lolli, and Adam had been sitting together since the beginning of the year. Zach had usually sat at a different table. Now he sat with them every day.

Usually there was no forgetting that, since he never stopped talking and joking around. But today he was being very quiet.

"What's wrong, Zach?" Janey asked, giving him a poke on the arm. "Aren't you excited that we helped another pet?"

Zach looked up. "Hip hip hooray," he said with a shrug. "I'm glad you found Leah's bird. But we haven't done anything to help Hall Cat yet."

Adam sipped his chocolate milk. "Yeah, it's too bad her owners weren't home yesterday when we went there."

"We'd better try again today," Zach said. "Let's meet up and go over there right after school."

"Veto," Janey said. "You guys can go

without me. I have to stay after school today for my flute lesson."

"Sorry, Zach, but I can't make it today, either," Lolli said. "I promised Brooke I'd take Roscoe to visit her grandma."

"Oh, right," Janey said. Lolli had told the whole group about her talk with Brooke. When Lolli had offered to help, Brooke had explained that her grandmother was a lifelong animal lover. Since Lolli was a member of the Pet Rescue Club, Brooke had asked if she knew any animals who could visit the old lady to cheer her up. Lolli had immediately volunteered to take her own dog, who was super friendly and loved going to new places.

Adam smiled. "The Pet Rescue Club is

already expanding," he said. "We started off as people helping animals. Now we're also animals helping people!"

Janey giggled. Adam didn't joke around nearly as much as Zach did, but the jokes he made were usually really funny.

"I guess that's true," Janey said. "After all, Roscoe is an honorary member, since he's one of our mascots. Maybe next time Mulberry can go for a visit!"

She glanced at Zach to see what he thought of that. But he didn't even seem to be listening.

He was looking at Adam. "I guess you can't come to Hall Cat's house right after school, either, right?" he said. "You probably have to take care of your clients."

"Right," Adam said. "I can come meet

you when I'm finished, though."

Lolli nodded. "I probably won't be at Brooke's grandma's house for that long," she said. "I'll come help with Hall Cat after I'm done, too."

"Me, three," Janey said. "I'll get my mom to drop me off there after my lesson."

"Okay." Zach looked a little happier. He reached for Janey's last carrot stick and popped it into his mouth. "You weren't going to eat that, were you?" he mumbled.

Zach stared out the living room window. He could see Hall Cat's house from there. He could also see Hall Cat. She was sleeping in her owners' driveway. Zach winced every time a car drove by, even though the cat wasn't that close to the road at the moment. But what if she decided to take a nap in the middle of the road next time?

Zach wondered how much longer it would be before his friends showed up. He'd lost his watch weeks ago, so he jumped up and hurried into the kitchen to check the clock on the microwave.

"No way!" he said out loud. He glanced at his oldest brother, who was fixing a sandwich. "Is that clock right?"

Josh glanced at him. "Why? Do you have an important business meeting?" Snorting with laughter, Josh picked up his sandwich and loped out of the kitchen.

Zach gritted his teeth. The clock had to be wrong! It was impossible that he'd only been home from school for half an hour. That meant his friends probably wouldn't be there for almost another hour!

He hurried back into the living room and looked outside. Hall Cat had woken up. She was sitting up and washing her paw.

"I can't wait any longer," Zach muttered. Yelling to his father that he was going out, he hurried across the street.

This time the baby's father opened the door again. His wife was sitting in a chair right behind him, trying to squeeze the baby's chubby foot into a tiny sock.

When the father saw Zach standing there holding Hall Cat, he sighed. "Hello again," he said. "Is Hall Cat getting into trouble?"

"Not yet," Zach said. "But she might if you keep putting her outside." He took a deep breath, trying to remember all the stuff Janey and the others had said, along with everything his mother had told him about outdoor cats when he'd tried to convince her that Mulberry wanted to go outside and chase mice. "She probably won't live as long being an outdoor cat. She could get hit by a car, or eat something poisonous, or get attacked by mean dogs or wild animals, or—"

"All right, all right," the father said. He sounded a little worried. "I know it's not ideal. But this is a safe neighborhood, and we're just trying to come up with a solution that works for everybody."

Zach took a step inside and set Hall Cat down on the floor. She wandered toward the baby and sniffed at his foot, which was dangling off the side of the chair.

"Careful, Hall Cat," the mother said. "Don't scare the baby." She glanced at her husband. "Put the cat back out, will you, honey?"

Zach didn't think the baby looked scared at all. He wondered if the woman had heard anything he'd just said. Zach's older brothers ignored him all the time, and Zach hated it. He was getting the same feeling now.

"Hall Cat's not scary, but I am!" he blurted out. Putting his thumbs in his ears, he waggled his fingers and made a funny face at the baby. "Ooga booga!"

He was only joking around, but the baby's face scrunched up. A second later he let out a loud wail.

"Oh, no!" the baby's mother exclaimed,

grabbing him and hugging him close. "It's okay, sweetie. Don't cry! Please, don't start crying again!"

"I'm sorry." Zach immediately felt guilty. "I was just kidding around. I didn't think that would actually scare him."

The father put a hand on his shoulder. "I know, kiddo. You couldn't know that the baby was up all night with an earache. We're all a little touchy right now, that's all."

"Sorry," Zach muttered again, feeling his face go red. "I guess I'll go."

The mother glanced up at him. "Yes, maybe you'd better," she said with a sigh. "Please take Hall Cat back outside on your way, all right?"

9

Roscoe Helps Out

Lolli was having a great time at Brooke's grandmother's house. Her father had met her in the car with Roscoe right after school. He'd dropped Lolli, Brooke, and Roscoe off at a tidy two-story house just a few blocks from Zach's place.

"Grandma's expecting us," Brooke had told Lolli as Mr. Simpson drove off. "She can't wait to meet Roscoe. She hasn't had a dog in a few years, but she loves them."

Brooke was right. Brooke's grandmother

had been thrilled to see them—especially Roscoe.

"Oh, aren't you a big lug of a fellow?" she'd cooed, walking out onto the front stoop to rub Roscoe all over. The dog had enjoyed every second of the attention, wiggling from head to foot with his tail wagging nonstop.

Finally the old woman had glanced up with a smile. She looked like an older version of Brooke, with friendly brown eyes behind wire-rimmed glasses.

"I'm sorry, where are my manners?" she'd exclaimed, ushering Lolli, Roscoe, and Brooke into her house. It was nice and cool inside, with lots of framed family photos decorating the walls and the scents of lavender and lemon in the air. "You must be Lolli. It's lovely to meet you. You can call me Grandma Madge if you like."

"Okay." Lolli smiled back, liking the woman already. "It's nice to meet you, too, Grandma Madge. This is Roscoe."

"Oh, I know." Grandma Madge rubbed the dog's ears. "Brookie told me all about both of you. Is it true you live on a farm?"

"Yes," Lolli said. "It's not a very big farm, but it's big enough for the three of us. My parents grow all kinds of organic vegetables, and sometimes they make cheese from our goats' and sheep's milk."

"Wonderful! Roscoe must love having a whole farm to patrol," Grandma Madge said.

Brooke flopped onto a comfortable-looking sofa. "Grandma loves big dogs," she told Lolli. "Isn't that right, Grandma?"

"Absolutely." Grandma Madge sat on a chair and patted her knees. Roscoe came over and laid his big, blocky head on the woman's lap. His tongue flopped out, and drool dribbled onto Grandma Madge's slacks.

"Oops," Lolli said. "Sorry about that. He drools when he's happy."

"Oh, don't be silly." The old woman

laughed. "What's a little drool among friends? Why, I once had a Saint Bernard who could sling drool farther than you could toss a ball…"

After that, she was off and running, telling the girls a whole series of stories about the dogs and cats she'd known throughout her long life. She'd always had at least one pet around for as long as she could remember.

"…and of course, Brookie remembers Muffin," she finished, glancing at her granddaughter.

Brooke nodded. "She was this awesome dog Grandma had when I was little," she told Lolli. "Muffin used to let me dress her up, even though she was even bigger than Roscoe."

Lolli laughed. "She sounds cool," she said. "What kind of dog was she?"

"Nobody was ever quite sure." Grandma Madge chuckled. "She was just this gorgeous big black-and-tan mixed breed who could shed enough fur in a week to make three new dogs. We used to take a survey at parties to see what mix of breeds people thought she might be. We got everything from Great Dane to German shepherd to giant schnauzer!"

"Whatever breeds she was, Muffin was the best," Brooke said.

"Yes, she was quite a dog," Grandma Madge agreed with a faraway look in her eyes. She fondled Roscoe's ears. "She passed on a few years ago now."

"Did you think about getting another

dog?" Lolli asked. "Or did you miss Muffin too much?"

"Oh, I missed her all right. And yes, I thought about getting another. But by then, I was feeling too old to handle another large dog."

"I tried to talk them into getting a smaller dog, like a beagle or something," Brooke put in. "Or maybe a cute little kitten from the shelter."

Grandma Madge nodded. "We did consider it, but my husband was starting to get unsteady on his feet around that time. It just didn't seem worth the risk of him tripping over a new pet." She sighed. "Plus, I'm not sure I have the energy anymore for a lively puppy or kitten."

"That's too bad," Lolli said. "I can't

imagine not having animals around." She thought about Leah's pet canary. "Did you think about getting a pet that doesn't run around the house?"

"You mean, like a bird or something?" Grandma Madge shrugged. "That just wouldn't be the same."

She looked sad for a moment. Then Roscoe reached up and slurped her face with his large tongue, knocking her glasses askew.

"Oh!" Lolli exclaimed as she reached for her dog. "Roscoe, no! Bad dog!"

But Grandma Madge was laughing as she took off her glasses and rubbed them on her shirt. "No, don't scold him," she told Lolli. "He's just doing what dogs do. And I love it!" She stuck her glasses back on and stroked Roscoe's head.

Lolli smiled, though she felt a little bit sad herself. Grandma Madge loved animals— that was obvious. It was too bad she'd been without a special pet of her own for so long.

But thinking about Leah's bird had reminded Lolli about the Pet Rescue Club. That made her remember that she'd promised to meet her friends to talk to Hall Cat's owners. She stood up.

"I'm sorry, I should probably go," she told Grandma Madge and Brooke. "But maybe Roscoe and I could stop by and visit again another time?"

"I'd love that." Grandma Madge hugged Roscoe. "Please, come by whenever you like." She winked. "You too, Lolli."

Soon Lolli was hurrying down the sidewalk. "I wonder if the others are already at Hall Cat's house," she said to Roscoe. "Should we go to Zach's house first to see if he's there, or…"

She let her voice trail off. Just ahead, Hall Cat's front door had just swung open. A second later, Zach stepped out, looking red-faced and upset as he clutched Hall Cat in his arms.

10
Lolli's Big Idea

"Zach!" Lolli rushed over as Zach stumbled toward the sidewalk, still holding Hall Cat. "What happened? Where are the others?"

"Not here yet," Zach said. Then he blinked. "Wait, yes they are."

Lolli looked around. Adam was hurrying down the sidewalk toward them. Janey was just climbing out of her mother's car at the curb.

"Sorry I'm late," Adam said breathlessly. He looked at Hall Cat. "Did you talk to her owners?"

"Sort of," Zach said.

Janey rushed up. "Hi, Roscoe," she greeted the dog as he jumped around happily. "What's going on, you guys? Oh! Hall Cat is still outside."

Zach nodded. "I tried talking to them," he said. "They didn't listen."

"Why didn't you wait for us?" Janey said. "Come on, let's go try again."

"I don't think that's a good idea." Zach stroked Hall Cat's back, making her purr. "They seem kind of, um, distracted right now."

Adam shook his head. "It seems like those people just don't have time for a pet," he said. "Cats are a little easier to take care of than dogs. But cats need attention, too!"

"I know, right?" Zach tickled Hall Cat under her chin. "Especially Hall Cat. She's so sweet! I wish I could take her home. I bet they would let me." He sighed. "Unfortunately, my parents definitely wouldn't let me."

Lolli stared at Hall Cat. Then she stared at her friends. She was starting to get an idea...

"I wish I could take Hall Cat home, too," Janey said. "But you know about my dad's allergies. Maybe you could take her, Adam?"

"Sorry, I can't," Adam said. "My family's landlord doesn't allow any pets. That's why I don't have a dog, remember?"

"Really?" Janey blinked at him. "Oh. I never knew that."

Zach rolled his eyes. "That's because you never stop talking long enough to listen to anybody else."

Janey looked wounded. "I do too!"

"Don't start arguing," Adam told them. "We're supposed to be figuring out a way to help Hall Cat, remember? Maybe Lolli could take her home. Her parents wouldn't even notice another animal on the farm, right?"

Zach brightened. "That's a great idea!"

"Lolli?" Janey poked Lolli on the shoulder. "Why aren't you saying anything?"

"I'm thinking," Lolli said. "I might have an idea for a way to help Hall Cat."

"Really?" Adam said. "You mean you thought of something to convince her people to keep her inside?"

Lolli shrugged. "No," she said. "But maybe that's not the point. Even if they kept her inside, they just don't seem that interested in her anymore."

"So you're going to ask your parents if you can keep her?" Zach asked.

"Me? No." Lolli smiled. "But I might know someone who would appreciate her a lot more than her owners do."

"Really? Who?" Janey asked.

Lolli pointed down the block. "Brooke's grandma," she said. "She loves animals, but she can't have a big dog or a hyper puppy or frisky kitten."

Zach glanced down at the cat purring in his arms. "Hall Cat isn't hyper."

"Right." Lolli smiled. "Come on, let's go ask her owners if they'd be willing to give her up to a good home."

When the baby's father answered the door, he looked annoyed at first. But when he heard the kids' question, he looked thoughtful.

"Do you really know someone who wants Hall Cat?" he asked, leaning down to give Roscoe a pat.

"We're not sure yet," Lolli said. "We need to ask her. But we wanted to get permission from you first."

The man reached out and scratched Hall Cat under the chin. "I suppose that would be all right," he said. "She deserves more attention than we have to give her right now. And I was thinking about what you kids were saying about her being safer living indoors. I'll miss her, though."

"You can still visit her," Janey told him. "The lady who might want her lives nearby."

"We'll come back and let you know what she says," Lolli promised.

Lolli led the others back to Grandma Madge's house. Brooke answered the door when they knocked. She looked surprised to see them.

"Oh," she said. "It's the whole Pet Rescue Club! Is that an animal you're rescuing?" She reached out to pat Hall Cat.

"Maybe," Lolli said with a smile. "Is Grandma Madge around?"

"I'm here, I'm here." Grandma Madge hurried up behind Brooke. "Oh! What a cute kitty. I've always loved black cats!"

Lolli traded a smile with her friends. "We're glad to hear that," she said. "Because Hall Cat happens to be looking for a new home."

Janey nodded. "She's super friendly."

"And she's not hyper," Zach added. "I doubt she'd ever trip anybody, no matter what her owners say."

Grandma Madge looked a little confused. "Her owners?"

Everyone started talking at once, telling Grandma Madge all about Hall Cat. Meanwhile Hall Cat herself started to wiggle in Zach's arms. He set her down on the stoop. Roscoe leaned forward to sniff at the cat, and she batted him on the nose with her paw. Then she strolled forward between Brooke and Grandma Madge—right into the house!

"Look," Janey said with a laugh. "She's making herself at home already!"

"You little rascal," Grandma Madge exclaimed. She picked up the cat, who immediately started purring. "Oh my, you are a cutie, aren't you?"

"I think she likes you," Lolli said.

Grandma Madge smiled down at the cat. "Yes. Well, I really wasn't planning on getting a pet. But…"

Lolli held her breath. Would Grandma Madge agree to take Hall Cat?

"You need company right now, Grandma," Brooke spoke up. "Maybe a cat like this would be perfect."

"Oh, I don't know, Brookie." Grandma Madge was still smiling. "I don't think I could ever live with a pet named Hall Cat."

"You—you couldn't?" Lolli's heart sank.

"Absolutely not." Grandma Madge winked at her. "The first thing I'll have to do is come up with a much nicer name."

It took Lolli a second to realize what she was saying. Then she heard Zach gasp.

"You mean you'll take her?" he cried.

"Why not?" Grandma Madge said. "As Brookie says, I could use the company. Until Roscoe came to visit, I didn't realize how much I'd missed having an animal around the house. And a nice, quiet older cat will be much easier to manage than a dog or a younger animal, especially once Grandpa comes home."

"Hooray!" Lolli cried. "Now the only thing left is to decide what to name her!"

"How about Halloween?" Zach said.

"Veto," Janey declared. "That's a goofy name. Why not just call her Hallie?"

"Hallie," Grandma Madge said thoughtfully. "You know, I think I like that."

"We should go back and tell her old owners the good news," Janey told her friends.

"Don't bother," Grandma Madge said, cuddling Hall Cat. "I know the young couple you mean. I'll walk down there myself and let them know." She smiled. "I've been wanting to see that sweet baby of theirs, anyway."

"Awesome!" Janey said. "I guess it's another happy ending for the Pet Rescue Club."

"This totally rules," Zach exclaimed.

"Yeah," Adam agreed.

Lolli didn't say anything for a second.

She was so happy she thought she might burst. The Pet Rescue Club had helped another animal! Better yet, they'd helped a person at the same time! She was sure Grandma Madge and Hall Cat—no, Hallie— would be much happier now that that the Pet Rescue Club had helped them find each other. She was pretty sure the baby's family would be happier, too.

"This is definitely a happy ending," Lolli said. "For everyone!"

Food for Thought

We share a lot with our pets: our lives, our homes, our love, our deepest secrets. But is it a good idea to share our food?

Not always. Several common foods that are perfectly safe for people can be dangerous or even deadly for our cats, dogs, and other pets. Also, there are some household items and houseplants that pets should never be allowed to chew on or eat. Here are a few examples, but check *aspca.org* for a more complete list.

- Onions and garlic
- Chocolate
- Coffee
- Avocado (especially dangerous to birds and rodents)
- Grapes and raisins
- Many human medications
- Antifreeze
- Fabric softener sheets
- Amaryllis
- Pothos (a popular houseplant)

The Benefits of Adopting a Senior Cat

Some vets consider a cat to be a "senior" when he or she reaches the age of seven. However, many house cats now live well into their twenties. There are a lot of reasons to adopt a senior cat. Here are just a few.

1. With a kitten, it takes a while before their full personality emerges, but with a senior cat you'll know right away if you're inviting a lap cat or a more independent cat into your home. You'll be more confident that you are selecting a good fit for your family when you choose a senior feline.

2. A senior cat is less likely to knock things over and break things or scratch on your good furniture than a kitten would be.

3. A senior cat will enjoy sitting near you when you read a book, do your homework, or watch TV.

4. A senior cat still has lots of playful energy.

Meet the Real Hallie!

Hall Cat, the kitty in this story, was inspired by a real-life animal rescue story. A black cat named Hallie was left at a shelter in Illinois when she was ten years old. Her previous owners said they didn't have time for her anymore. Luckily, she was adopted by someone who appreciates older cats, and has been a wonderful partner for her new owner ever since!

The Lonely Pony

by Catherine Hapka
illustrated by Dana Regan

At the Shelter

"Oh my gosh, this bunny has to be the cutest animal I've ever seen!" Lolli Simpson exclaimed.

She was in the lobby of the Third Street Animal Shelter with her friends Janey Whitfield and Zach Goldman. The three of them were watching Zach's mother examine a fluffy black-and-white rabbit who was a new shelter resident. Dr. Goldman was a veterinarian with a busy private practice. But she made time each week to donate her skills to the shelter.

Zach looked at Lolli and grinned. "Really?" he said. "Cuter than Roscoe?"

Roscoe was Lolli's dog. He was part Lab, part Rottweiler, and part who-knew-what.

Lolli smiled at Zach. "Okay, the bunny is one of the cutest animals I've ever seen," she said.

But she knew Zach was only teasing her. He loved to joke around and play pranks.

Janey reached out and stroked the rabbit's fur. "He's so soft," she said. "I've never seen a rabbit at the shelter before."

"We do get some in from time to time," said Kitty, the kids' favorite shelter worker. She was a lively young woman with a blonde ponytail. "They can be a little tricky to adopt out."

"Why?" Lolli giggled as the rabbit's little nose twitched. "He's adorable! I already want to take him home myself."

"If Lolli doesn't adopt him, maybe the Pet Rescue Club can help find this bun bun a home," Zach said.

The Pet Rescue Club was a group the three kids had started, along with their friend Adam Santos. The four of them tried to help needy animals in any way they could.

"How did he end up here, anyway?" Lolli asked Kitty. "I can't believe anyone would give up such a sweet pet."

Kitty sighed. "This little guy's previous owners bought him on a whim last Easter," she said. "They thought having a cute little bunny hopping around their house would be fun. But they weren't prepared for how much work a pet like this can be."

"So they took him to the shelter?" Janey said with a frown. "That's vile."

Vile was Janey's new favorite word. She liked to use interesting or unusual words whenever she could.

"How much work could a little bunny like this be?" Lolli wiggled her nose at the rabbit, then smiled as he wiggled his nose in return.

Dr. Goldman glanced up from examining the rabbit's long, floppy ears. "Actually, rabbits require somewhat specialized care," she said. "They need safe housing, and they do best with certain types of foods, and of course every species has its own health and behavior issues."

"Okay, I get it." Lolli tickled the bunny under the chin. "But it would be worth it to have such a cutie pie around the farm! I think I'll ask my parents if I can adopt him."

"Really? That would be fab." Janey looked a little bit wistful, and Lolli knew exactly why. Janey's father was severely allergic to animals, so Janey couldn't have any pets at home. That was how the Pet Rescue Club had come to be. Janey had started a blog asking people to share their cutest pet photos. Someone had posted a picture of a sad, neglected dog named Truman. Janey and her friends had helped Truman find a new home with their homeroom teacher, Ms. Tanaka. The rest was history!

Dr. Goldman gave the bunny one last pat, then stepped back. "He seems healthy," she told Kitty.

"Great. I'll take him back to his cage." Kitty picked up the rabbit, who snuggled into her arms. "Lolli, if you really think you might like to adopt him, we can talk about rabbits' special needs later."

"Okay, thanks," Lolli said. "I need to ask my parents first."

"It'll be cool if you get a pet rabbit,"

Janey said after Kitty had left with the rabbit and Dr. Goldman had gone into the dog room to check on a patient. "I wonder if we could teach him some tricks."

"Yeah, like riding my skateboard!" Zach said with a laugh. "Wait, can rabbits walk on a leash like dogs do? Maybe Adam should expand his business to include walking rabbits, too!"

Adam had a successful pet-sitting and dog-walking business, even though he was only nine. He was a good dog trainer, too. He'd helped Truman learn how to behave better before Ms. Tanaka adopted him.

Janey frowned. "Speaking of Adam, where is he?" She checked her pink watch. "He was supposed to be here ten minutes ago for our meeting."

"I'm sure he'll be here soon," Lolli said. "Saturday is always a busy day for pet sitting. I think he said he had to walk a few dogs after lunch."

"Well, I hope he hurries up and gets here." Janey sounded impatient. "We need to figure out how to find more animals to help, and the weekend's almost half over already!"

Zach pointed at the shelter's front door. "Your wish is our command," he said. "Here comes Adam now."

Adam hurried in. "Sorry I'm late," he said breathlessly. "But I have to tell you guys about—"

"We thought you'd never get here!" Janey interrupted loudly. "I was about to start the meeting without you."

"Okay," Adam said. "But—"

"This is a very important meeting, you know," Janey went on. "Nobody has contacted us since we helped that cat, Hallie, last week. I'm sure there are lots of animals that need our help, but we can't help them if we don't know about them, right? So I was thinking, maybe we should write something on my blog asking people to look for needy animals and e-mail us, or—"

"Janey!" Adam broke in. His voice was

louder than usual. "If you'd let me get two words in, that's what I want to tell you!"

Janey looked surprised at being interrupted. "Huh?"

Adam took a deep breath. "I think I found an animal that needs our help," he said, his voice its normal volume again. "I've noticed her a couple of times while I was out walking dogs. And today I made a special trip to see if she's still there—that's why I was a little late."

"Really?" Lolli said. "What kind of animal is it, Adam? Another dog?"

Adam shook his head. "Definitely not a dog."

"A cat?" Janey said. "Or maybe a rabbit?"

"I bet it's an injured Bigfoot," Zach joked.

Adam just shook his head again. "Come with me and I'll show you," he said.

2

A New Mission

"Are we going to my house?" Lolli joked, peering out the car window.

Dr. Goldman smiled at her in the rearview mirror. "I don't know," she said. "Adam? Should we turn down Lolli's road?"

"No, keep going straight," Adam said. "It's about a mile farther that way."

The Pet Rescue Club had asked Zach's mother to drive them to see Adam's mystery pet. Dr. Goldman had agreed, since she was finished working for the day. She was just as curious to see Adam's mystery animal as everyone else!

Adam had directed them to a rural area right outside of town. Lolli lived nearby on a small farm with her parents, where they grew organic vegetables and kept a sheep and a couple of goats. There were lots of other farms in the area, too. Some grew crops like corn or soybeans. But Janey preferred the ones with cows, horses, or other animals grazing in the fields. There was even a llama farm! Among the farms were some regular houses with extra-large yards.

"Are we there yet?" Janey asked after another few minutes of driving.

"Almost." Adam pointed. "There—turn right onto that road."

Dr. Goldman turned onto a narrow, winding road with no sidewalks or street lamps. There were only a few houses in sight. After a short distance, Adam told her to pull over.

"Is this it?" Janey asked as everyone climbed out of the car.

She looked around. Beside the road was a rickety fence, built half of wood and half of wire. It enclosed a small pen that was choked with weeds. There was a small, tumbledown shed in the middle and a plastic trough half-filled with slimy, greenish water near the gate. On the hillside beyond the pen was a much larger, grassy pasture where a small herd of dairy cows were grazing peacefully.

"Are we here to rescue those cows?" Zach joked. "Because I don't think they'll fit in the dog runs at the shelter."

"Not exactly," Adam said. "The animal

we need to help is right in here."

He waved at the small pen. Janey looked at it again. The only animals she could see in there were some flies buzzing above the water tank.

"Where's the pet who needs rescuing?" Lolli asked. "I don't see anything."

"The animal I saw is probably in that shed." Adam leaned on the fence and whistled loudly.

"I knew it!" Janey said. "It is a dog, isn't it? Adam, I've heard you whistle like that to your clients a million times!"

But Lolli gasped and pointed. "It's not a dog," she cried. "Look!"

An animal had just stepped into view from behind the shed. Janey could hardly believe her eyes. Could that really be...

"Oh my gosh!" she cried. "It's a horse!"

"No way." Zach climbed on the lowest rung of the fence for a better look. "It looks like it shrunk in the wash!"

Lolli smiled. "It's not a horse," she said. "It's a pony!"

Adam looked confused. "You mean a baby horse?"

"Not quite," Dr. Goldman said with a smile.

"A lot of people think a pony is a baby horse. But a pony is actually a horse below a certain height, or sometimes it's a certain breed."

The animal stepped farther out from behind the shed. Whatever you called her, she was the smallest equine Janey had ever

seen! The pony pricked her little ears, then let out a high-pitched whinny and trotted toward them.

"Aw, she's coming to see us!" Janey said. "Here, pony pony!"

"Careful, kids," Dr. Goldman said. "Some ponies bite."

Janey hardly heard her. The pony reached the fence and stuck her muzzle through the wire. When Janey touched the pony's nose, it felt as soft as velvet.

"She's so cute!" Lolli exclaimed.

"Yeah," Adam said. "But look—her mane and tail are all messed up."

Janey saw that he was right. There were brambles tangled in the pony's thick mane and tail. Her hair looked even more snarled than Janey's did after swimming.

"She does look a bit neglected," Dr. Goldman said, peering through the fence at the pony's feet. "Her hooves are long and chipped. And her coat's not in great condition, either."

Janey glanced at the vet. "Wow, you know a lot about ponies! I thought you only treated cats and dogs and other regular pets."

"You're right, I do specialize in small animals." Dr. Goldman shrugged. "But I studied the basics of taking care of large animals in vet school, so I know a little." She reached into her pocket and pulled out a piece of hard candy. "For instance, I learned that most equines love peppermints!"

She unwrapped the candy and held it out, her hand flat with the palm facing up. The pony lipped it up and crunched it.

"You're right, she loves it!" Janey exclaimed. "I think she wants more."

The pony stretched her head over the fence as far as she could. Her ears swiveled back and forth excitedly, and she let out an eager nicker.

Dr. Goldman laughed. "Sorry, girl, that's the only one I have."

Adam smiled, too, but he looked worried. "I've seen this pony in this field every day since I started walking a dog near here last week," he said. "But I've never seen any-one out here feeding her or brushing her or anything."

"Really?" Janey said. "That's totally vile. What if she's been abandoned?"

Lolli gasped. "Abandoned? We have to help her!"

"Let's not jump to conclusions, kids," Dr. Goldman said. "Ponies can get awfully messy in a short time. Maybe she's been rolling in the brambles, and nobody has been by to groom her yet today."

"Come on, Mom," Zach said. "If my hair looked like that, you'd have it tidied up lickety-split." He grinned. "No matter how fast I tried to run away!"

That made everyone laugh, including Dr. Goldman. "I suppose it wouldn't hurt to ask around."

Janey said, "Okay, let's go!"

"Hold on." Dr. Goldman put a hand on Janey's arm. "I'm not sure we should wander around knocking on strangers' doors."

"But we have to do something!" Lolli exclaimed. "We need to help this poor pony!"

"We will," Dr. Goldman said. "I was just going to say, a few of my clients live around here. We could see if any of them are home, and ask if they know who owns her. All right?"

Janey smiled. She should have known Dr. Goldman wouldn't let them down!

"All right!" she exclaimed. "The Pet Rescue Club is on the job! So, let's go!"

Lola's Story

The first house they tried was a tidy farmhouse with a big front porch right next to the pony's pen. When Dr. Goldman knocked on the door, the sound of excited yapping came from inside.

"Wow," Adam said. "It sounds like these people have a lot of dogs."

"Five," Dr. Goldman said with a smile. "The Valentines love dogs. They're among my best clients."

A moment later, a plump, pleasant-looking man opened the door. He was in his late sixties, with a bushy gray mustache. Five little dogs danced around his legs.

"Dr. Goldman!" the man exclaimed with a smile. "What a nice surprise! Look, gang, your doctor's here!"

"Oh, your dogs are so cute!" Janey blurted out, bending to pat them as they leaped excitedly around her.

"Hello, Tom," Dr. Goldman said. "Sorry to bother you on a Saturday."

"No bother at all!" He beamed at her. "What can I do for you, doc?"

"We noticed the pony in the pen over there," Dr. Goldman said. "Do you happen to know who owns her?"

The man looked surprised. "As a matter of fact, we do. Her name is Lola."

"Really?" Lolli giggled. "That sounds almost like my name!"

Meanwhile, Janey traded a surprised look with Adam. Mr. Valentine seemed really nice, and his dogs looked happy and healthy. He definitely didn't seem like the type of person who would mistreat a pony on purpose. What was going on?

"This is Lolli, Tom," Dr. Goldman said.

"She's practically your neighbor—her family lives on one of the farms over on Crooked Tree Road." She went on to introduce the other three kids.

"Nice to meet you all," the man said. "I'm Tom Valentine."

"Tom?" a woman's voice called from inside. "Who is at the door?"

A moment later the woman appeared. She was just as plump and pleasant looking as her husband, with wavy hair and bright blue eyes.

"This is my wife, Val," Tom told the kids. "Val, Dr. Goldman and her friends were asking about Lola."

"I didn't realize you two had a pony," Dr. Goldman said. "Have you had her long?"

"Just a few months," Val said. "Why don't you have a seat on the porch and I'll fetch some lemonade. Then we can tell you all about her."

A few minutes later, Dr. Goldman and the Pet Rescue Club members were settled in comfortable wicker furniture with tart, tasty glasses of lemonade. The little dogs were there, too. Two of them were snuggled in Janey's lap. Zach was playing fetch with a third, while the other two took turns running back and forth between Lolli and Adam.

"So," Janey said, scratching one of the dogs behind his silky ears. "Where did you get Lola?"

"She came from the racetrack," Val said.

Zach laughed. "What? That tiny pony

was a racehorse? No way!"

"With those short legs, she must have lost every race," Lolli said with a giggle.

Val laughed, too. "No, Lola wasn't a racehorse, but she lived with one."

"That's right," Tom said. "You see, Lola was a stall companion to a thoroughbred racehorse named Red."

"A stall companion?" Janey wrinkled her nose. "What's that?"

"She was there to keep Red company," Val explained. "All the sights and sounds of the track made him nervous, but having Lola in the stall with him kept him much calmer and happier."

Dr. Goldman nodded. "I know what you mean. Part of my clinical work in vet school took me to the racetrack. On one of my visits there I vaccinated and dewormed a goat who was the companion to a pretty successful racehorse."

"Wow," Janey said. She'd never heard of such a thing! "So why isn't Lola still at the racetrack helping Red?"

"Because Red retired from racing a few months ago," Val said, taking a sip of her lemonade. "His owners gave him to a young local woman who retrains racehorses for new careers as riding horses."

"I've heard about that," Lolli said. "My parents donated some hay to a group that helps racehorses find new homes after they're retired."

"Yes, well, this young woman does marvelous work," Tom said. "At least that's what Red's old racing trainer tells me. Unfortunately, Red's new trainer wasn't able to take Lola. And his old race trainer had no use for Lola once Red was gone, since none of his other horses needed a companion."

"Poor Lola," Adam said.

"Yeah," Zach said. "She got laid off from her job, and had nowhere to go."

"Exactly." Tom poured everyone a little

more lemonade. "The race trainer is an old fishing buddy of mine, and he knows that Val and I are animal lovers." He smiled and bent to pat one of the little dogs. "Obviously!"

"Tom had also mentioned to him how I loved reading horse books as a child," Val put in. "So he asked if we'd be interested in having Lola." She sighed. "The trouble is, he didn't tell us just how much time, money, and hard work it takes to keep a horse—even a small one!"

Tom nodded. "We just can't keep up with it all," he said. "Not with my bad knees and Val's busy volunteering schedule. We've been meaning to ask around for help, but haven't quite found the time."

Janey bit her lip and glanced at her

friends. It sounded as if Tom and Val had meant to do a nice thing by taking Lola in. But they'd gotten in over their heads.

"I see," Dr. Goldman said with a sympathetic smile. "Did you ask the trainer to take her back?"

"He can't," Tom said. "He suggested we ask around town to see if anyone wants poor old Lola."

"You don't have to do that," Janey blurted out. " We can do that for you! The Pet Rescue Club will help you find Lola the perfect new home!"

4

Project Pony

Val looked surprised. "The what club?" she said. "Oh, but never mind—I don't want to bother you kids with our problems."

Her husband smiled at Janey and the others. "Yes, we'll work it out."

"No, really!" Zach said. "We have a club that helps pets find new homes and stuff."

"They really do," Dr. Goldman said with a nod. "They've helped several local pets already." She told the couple about Truman and the other animals the Pet Rescue Club had helped.

Val looked impressed. "How wonderful! What do you think, Tom? Maybe they can help us after all."

"We definitely can," Janey said. "Lola is so cute, I'm sure it won't take long at all to find her the perfect new home."

"What a relief," Val exclaimed. "See, we're scheduled to leave on a road trip in about a week to visit our son. He lives out of state, so we were planning to stay for a couple of weeks."

"That's right," Tom added. "We were worried we'd have to hurry to find something to do with Lola before we leave."

"Well, now you don't have to worry," Janey said. "Not with the Pet Rescue Club on the job." She knew they would have to work fast to find Lola a new home before the Valentines left on their trip next week. But she was sure they could do it.

"Terrific," Tom said. "Can you take her today?"

"Today?" Janey gulped and glanced at the others. "Um…"

"We could call the shelter and see if they can take Lola in," Lolli suggested.

"Yeah." Zach grinned. "She's not any bigger than a Great Dane or something. She'd totally fit in one of the large dog runs!"

"Well, I've never seen a horse there, but I suppose it wouldn't hurt to ask." Dr. Goldman dug into her pocket. "Here, you can use my cell phone."

Janey took the phone and dialed the familiar number. When Kitty answered, she explained the situation.

"We were hoping you could keep Lola at the shelter until we find her a home," Janey finished. "It probably won't take long."

"I'm sorry, Janey," Kitty said. "I'm afraid we don't have the facilities to take care of farm animals—not even small ones. I could call the shelter over in Lakeville for you, though. They have a couple of goats and a potbellied pig there right now, and I'm pretty sure they've taken in horses in the past."

"Lakeville?" Janey clutched the phone to her ear. "But that's almost an hour's drive away! How can we help her if she's not even close by?"

"What?" Zach whispered loudly, poking her on the arm. "What's she saying? What was that about Lakeville?"

"Ssh!" Janey hushed him. Kitty was talking again. "I'm sorry, could you repeat that? Zach was yapping in my ear."

Kitty chuckled. "I said, I could ask around about finding a foster home—maybe one of the farms outside of town could keep her for a few days."

"That sounds good. Hang on, let me tell the others." Janey lowered the phone. "Kitty says maybe she can help us find a foster home for Lola. She thinks one of the farms around here might be willing to take her in until we find her a permanent home."

"That's a good idea," Dr. Goldman said, and the Valentines nodded.

But Lolli gasped. "Wait," she exclaimed. "I live on a farm!"

Janey blinked at her. "Um, yeah, we

know." Then she gasped, too. "Wait! Are you saying—"

"What if I'm the foster home?" Lolli cried before Janey could finish. "Me and my parents, I mean. We have plenty of room in our pasture. And we already have the goats and sheep, so a tiny little horse wouldn't even be that much extra trouble."

"Perfect! I'll tell Kitty," Janey said.

"Wait," Dr. Goldman stopped her. Then she turned to Lolli. "I think we need to ask your parents about this. Do they have any experience taking care of horses?"

"I don't think so," Lolli said. "But they've had lots of other animals."

Zach's mom still looked dubious. "I know. But horses are a lot of work—more than most animals. You have to be careful about what you feed them, and they need their feet trimmed back every couple of months or so...."

"Yes, that's right," Val put in. "We never did get around to finding anyone to do the foot trimming."

Tom nodded. "Been meaning to call the race trainer to ask for his help, but he's awfully hard to reach."

"We won't have Lola long enough to worry about that sort of stuff," Janey told Dr. Goldman. "It'll just be for a few days."

Dr. Goldman scratched her chin. "Well, I suppose it's up to your parents," she told Lolli. "You'd better call them and see if they want to take this on."

"Kitty? We might know about a foster farm," Janey said into the phone. "We'll call you back in a minute, okay?" She hung up and handed the phone to Lolli. "Call your parents right now. I'm sure they'll say yes!" She crossed her fingers as her friend took the phone.

Soon Lolli was talking to her father. She told him about Lola and what Kitty had said about finding a foster home. "She wouldn't be any trouble at all," she finished. "The Pet Rescue Club would do all the work to take care of her. It will probably only be for a day or two."

Janey couldn't hear what Mr. Simpson said. But when Lolli hung up, she was smiling. "Dad said it's okay as long as we do all the work."

"Oh, thank you!" Val exclaimed. "I can't tell you what a load off our minds this is, kids."

Janey grinned at her. "You're welcome. I'll call Kitty and tell her."

When Janey hung up a moment later, Dr. Goldman stood up. "Thanks for the lemonade, Tom and Val," she said. "We'd better get going if we want to get Lola settled in tonight."

"Yeah, let's go tell her the good news!" Zach exclaimed. He raced off down the porch steps. The little dogs all barked and raced after him.

"Come back, you rascals!" Tom whistled loudly, and the dogs turned around and ran back to him.

Adam patted a couple of them. "They're well trained," he said admiringly.

"And cute." Janey grabbed the smallest dog for one last snuggle. "Thanks for the lemonade, Mr. and Mrs. Valentine. We'd better go get Lola!"

"We'll come along and say good-bye," Val said. "Just let us put the dogs in the house first."

Janey waited impatiently while the couple herded the excited dogs back inside. Then the whole group hurried back down the road.

When they arrived at the pen, Lola was

still standing by the fence. "Look, she was waiting for us," Lolli said.

"She must have known we were coming back to get her," Zach said. "Come on, it's time to go to your new foster farm!"

Adam blinked. "Yeah, but wait," he said. "How are we going to get her there?"

5

Travel Plans

Janey didn't know why her friends looked so worried. "It's not very far to Lolli's farm," she said. "And Lola is little. Why can't we just put her in the back of the car? That's how we'd carry a dog the same size, right?"

Dr. Goldman glanced at her hatchback, which was still parked beside the road. "Uh, I don't think so," she said. "Lola may be small, but she's not a dog. Her hooves will make a mess of my upholstery."

"Yeah." Zach grinned. "Besides, horses aren't house-trained."

"Don't you mean car-trained?" Lolli joked.

Janey looked at Val and Tom. "How do you take her places?" she asked.

"We don't." Tom shrugged. "My race-track friend dropped her off here with a big horse trailer."

"Oh." Janey bit her lip. "Well, maybe we can find someone with a pickup truck we could borrow. Lola could jump into the back and ride over that way."

Adam looked alarmed. "That doesn't sound very safe for Lola," he said. "What if she jumps out while we're driving?"

"We could ride back there with her and hold her in," Zach suggested.

"No," Dr. Goldman said immediately. "Out of the question. That would be much too dangerous."

Tom sighed. "Sorry, kids. Maybe we need to leave Lola to the experts after all. The shelter in Lakeville might have a trailer they can use to pick her up."

"No!" Lolli's eyes filled with tears. "I

really want her to come to my house."

"I understand, dear," Val said kindly. "But if we can't get her there…"

Janey frowned. Why did this have to be so complicated? All they needed to do was transport Lola a mile or so down the road….

"I've got it!" she blurted out. "We can do it the old-fashioned way."

"You mean hitch Lola up to a wagon and drive her back that way?" Zach said. "Cool!"

Janey shook her head. "We don't need a wagon," she said. "We can just walk her to Lolli's place."

"I suppose we could, at that," Dr. Goldman said. "It's not very far. Probably less than a mile."

Tom looked relieved. "I think we have a halter and lead rope around here somewhere.

Let me take a look."

He let himself into the pen. Lola followed him halfway to the shed, but when Zach called her name the pony returned to the kids.

Janey patted Lola as Tom disappeared into the shed. A minute later he emerged holding a tangle of dingy straps.

"Found it!" he called, hurrying back. "Now, if I can just remember how to put this thing on…"

"I think I can help." Dr. Goldman smiled and let herself into the pen. "At least I learned that much about horses in vet school!"

It only took her and Tom a moment to figure out how to put on and latch the pony's halter. Then Tom clipped the lead rope to the metal ring beneath Lola's chin.

"There you are, Lola." He gave the pony a pat. "Ready to go to your new foster home?"

Adam held the gate open as Lola followed Tom toward it. As soon as she went through, she yanked her head down and started nibbling on the long grass at the edge of the road.

"Looks like she's hungry," Lolli said.

Tom gave a tug on the lead rope. "Come on, Lola. You can eat when you get to Lolli's place."

The pony ignored him and kept eating. "Here, let me try," Zach said, grabbing the rope. He tried to pull Lola's head up, but it stayed where it was. "Wow, she's stronger than she looks!"

"Come on, Lola," Janey cooed, leaning closer. "Don't you want to come with us?"

"Yeah, you'll love Lolli's place," Adam added. "Come on, girl!" He let out a whistle.

That got Lola's attention. She lifted her head to look at Adam. At the same time, Zach gave another tug on the rope. The pony took a step forward.

"It's working!" Janey cried. "Keep going!"

Zach walked a few steps. Lola followed him.

"Good luck, kids," Tom called. "We'll stop over in a little while with her leftover hay and things."

"Great," Dr. Goldman said. "Maybe you can give me a ride back to my car then."

She started giving the Valentines directions to Lolli's house. Janey kept moving, staying beside Lola and urging her to keep walking.

For a while, Lola seemed willing to let the kids lead her along beside the road. But then she spotted a tasty patch of clover and lowered her head again.

"Lola, no!" Lolli cried. "We'll never get there if you stop to eat every few steps."

Dr. Goldman caught up and helped the

kids get Lola moving again. But once again, the pony stopped after a minute or two to eat more grass.

"How does anyone ever get a horse anywhere?" Janey exclaimed.

"Most horses must not be as hungry as Lola," Lolli guessed.

Zach grinned. "Now I know why there's no grass growing on racetracks," he said. "All the horses would just run out of the starting gate and start eating!"

"Actually, I saw a racetrack on TV once that was grass," Adam said.

Janey frowned at them. "Would you stop talking about racetracks and help keep Lola moving? Otherwise this will take all night!"

"Sorry," Adam said. "Lola—heel! Heel,

girl!" He patted his leg, like he did to signal a dog to follow him.

But Lola ignored him. "She's not a dog, Adam," Janey said. "She probably doesn't know what 'heel' means."

"Is there another word they use to get

horses to heel?" Lolli wondered. "Gallop, Lola! Trot!"

The pony didn't respond except to move a step forward to a nicer patch of grass. Janey sighed and wiped her forehead. It was a warm afternoon, and she was starting to sweat.

"We haven't gone very far," Dr. Goldman said. "Do you want to turn back and tell the Valentines this isn't going to work?"

That made Janey forget all about how hot she was. "No!" she said. "We'll get her there." Glancing at Lola, she muttered, "Eventually."

6

Special Needs

Eventually, they made it. It took a long time, but finally the Pet Rescue Club reached Lolli's long gravel driveway. The kids had taken turns leading Lola, and it was Janey's turn right then. She kept the pony in the middle of the drive so she wouldn't be tempted to try to eat the grass growing alongside it. Lola looked from side to side as she walked. Janey guessed that the pony was checking out the orchard of fruit trees on one side of her and the big fenced-in pasture on the other side.

Lolli's parents were waiting halfway up the driveway, with Roscoe sitting beside them. The family's sheep and two goats were right on the other side of the fence nearby, staring curiously at the new arrivals.

When Roscoe spotted the pony, he jumped up and barked. His tail wagged, and he tried to run forward. But Lolli's father had

him on a leash, and held him back.

"We were just getting worried," Lolli's mother called. "Oh, that pony is adorable!"

"I know, right?" Lolli said. "She doesn't like walking on a leash, though."

"Yeah," Zach said. "She definitely needs a few training sessions with Adam."

"Never mind that." Now that they had arrived, Janey couldn't wait to get into a nice, air-conditioned house and have a snack. "Let's put her in the pasture and then go take a rest."

"Not so fast," Dr. Goldman said. "You can't just toss her in a pasture."

"Why not?" Zach said. "Isn't that where horses live?"

"Yes, but Lola has been in that small, weedy pen for a few months now," Dr. Goldman reminded the kids. "She's not used to eating lots of nice, rich grass. In vet school, we learned that horses' stomachs are surprisingly delicate. Eating too much really nice grass right now could make Lola very sick."

Janey was surprised. She'd never heard about anything like that. But she trusted Dr. Goldman.

"Besides, there could also be some weeds out there that she shouldn't eat," Lolli's mother said.

Adam glanced at the sheep and goats. "But those guys eat out there all the time."

"Yes, but sheep and goats have very different digestive systems from ponies," Dr. Goldman said. "They can eat a lot of weeds and plants that would poison Lola."

Janey's heart sank. "So what can we do to keep Lola safe?" she asked. "I don't want her to eat something poisonous!"

"We have some extra fencing stuff in the barn," Lolli's father spoke up. "You kids could build her a little pen inside the pasture."

"That's a great idea." Dr. Goldman smiled at him. "If you build it in a spot where the grass is a little sparser, Lola can graze safely without being able to eat too much rich stuff. And you can make it small enough to check for any possibly dangerous weeds and remove any you find."

"And feed them to the goats," Zach added, scratching one of the goats over the fence.

Janey sighed, glancing at the house. Her stomach rumbled.

But Janey wanted to help Lola, and that meant her empty stomach would have to wait. "Okay," she said, squaring her shoulders. "Let's build a pen."

Lolli's father helped the kids fetch some step-in fence posts and a couple of rolls of woven wire. "This stuff might not hold a full-sized horse," he said, scratching his head uncertainly. "But it should be good enough for a pony like Lola."

Lolli's mother put Roscoe in the house. Then she returned and held Lola's lead rope, letting the pony nibble on the short grass beside the driveway while her husband, Dr. Goldman, and the kids got to work on the fence. Before long Janey was sweating more than ever. Building fences was hard work!

But every time she wanted to quit, she

just looked over at Lola. That made her work even harder.

It took a long time, but finally the pen was ready. They'd built it along one side of the barn, where there was a deep overhang that Lola could use for shelter if the sun got too strong.

"Perfect!" Lolli's father declared at last. "Want to check it out, Lola?"

Dr. Goldman led the pony into the pen. She took off the lead rope and left Lola to explore.

Lola sniffed at the gate as Lolli shut it. Then she turned and looked around the pen. The goats and sheep were standing in their pasture on the other side of Lola's new fence, looking in. Lola whinnied at them, then trotted over to say hello through the wire. After that, she started to graze on her side of the fence, while the other animals nibbled the grass on their side.

Dr. Goldman smiled. "Ponies and horses are herd animals. Lola is probably happy to have company after being by herself for a couple of months."

"Maybe we can find her a home with other ponies," Adam said.

"Yeah." Janey glanced at Lolli's house. "Since Lola is having a snack, maybe it's time for us to have one, too?"

"Soon," Lolli's mother said. "You still need to set up a tub with water. And there's not much grass in the pen—won't we need hay?"

"The Valentines are bringing the supplies they have." Dr. Goldman shaded her hand against the late afternoon sun and peered down the driveway. "A-ha! Here they are, right on cue!"

A moment later, an SUV pulled to a stop nearby. Tom hopped out of the driver's seat. "Oh, look at that!" he exclaimed as he saw Lola. "She's found some friends."

The back of the SUV was crammed with hay bales, and there was a big, black tub for water in the backseat. "Come on, kids," Dr. Goldman said. "Let's get this stuff unloaded."

Half an hour later, Janey was so exhausted she wanted to lie down on the grass and take a nap. She and her friends had hauled the heavy bales of hay into the barn. They'd dragged the water tub into the pen, then hooked up the hose to fill it. They'd opened one of the hay bales and carried part of it out for Lola to eat. They'd found a spare shelf in the barn to store the grooming tools, a spare halter, and a few other items Tom had brought.

Meanwhile, Dr. Goldman had left with Tom, promising to return with her car to drive them all home. Janey couldn't wait!

But when she looked at Lola and saw her nibbling hay or grass, or sipping water, Janey felt happy and satisfied. "Lola is so cute," she told Lolli as they watched the pony. "I'm sure it won't take long to find her the perfect new home."

Lolli nodded, looking just as tired as Janey felt. "I'm glad she's here, even if she's a lot of work."

Janey giggled. "After this, taking care of Roscoe will seem super easy! Oh, and your new bunny, too, if you get him."

"Yeah." Lolli shot a look at her parents, who were helping the boys put away the hose. "Still, I think I'll wait and ask if I can get the bunny until after Lola goes to her new home."

7

Barn Chores

"Here we are, Farmer Janey," Janey's father joked as he pulled into Lolli's driveway the next day. "Better get going on your chores!"

Janey smiled. "Thanks for the ride, Daddy."

She jumped out of the car. Adam and Zach were already there with Lolli, watching Lola eat grass in her pen. They'd come straight over after Adam's morning dog-walking jobs.

"You're late," Zach called when he spotted Janey. "But don't worry, we saved all the stinky pony manure for you."

"Gee, thanks." Janey rolled her eyes.

"How's Lola?"

"Great," Lolli said. "After we feed her and clean up her pen, maybe we can use those brushes Mr. Valentine sent to groom her."

Janey nodded. "Good idea. We want her to look good for her photo session."

"What photo session?" Adam asked.

Janey held up her tablet. "I want to take some pictures of her to put on the blog. That will help her find a home faster."

"Good idea." Lolli picked up a pitchfork. "But first, let's get to work."

The kids worked hard. They cleaned up all the manure Lola had made overnight, using the pitchfork to put it in a wheelbarrow and then dumping it in the compost pile behind the barn. They scrubbed out the water tub and filled it again. They put out more hay.

"Okay." Lolli brushed hay off her hands. "Now for the fun part!"

She hurried into the barn and fetched the bucket of grooming tools. There were several brushes, a wide-toothed comb, a hoof pick, and a bottle of spray-on conditioner.

"Get ready for your beauty treatment, Lola!" Janey sang out as the kids entered the pen.

Lola was eating the pile of hay the kids had set out. She barely looked up when they started brushing her.

"Good girl," Janey said. "You want to look pretty, don't you?"

Adam leaned over to peer at the pony's

tangled mane. "I think I'll try getting some of these burrs out."

"Good idea," Janey said. "Her mane looks totally vile."

She handed Adam the comb. He grabbed it and got to work.

After close to an hour, the pony looked much better. Janey stepped back to survey their work.

"She looks great," she said. "See if you can get her to keep her head up so I can get some good pictures."

They spent the next several minutes on the photo shoot. It wasn't easy, since the pony preferred eating over posing. But finally Janey got some cute photos of Lola.

"Want me to upload them for you?" Zach offered.

Janey nodded and handed over the tablet. Zach knew just about everything about computers and technology, so she knew he'd do a good job of cropping and positioning the photos.

"Thanks," she said. "You can upload the

text I wrote, too, okay?" She pointed out the file on the desktop.

"Sure," Zach said as he got to work.

Lolli peered over his shoulder. "What'd you write?" she asked.

"Just a short entry about Lola," Janey said. "I did it last night after dinner. Zach can read it to you when it posts."

A second later, Zach cleared his throat and started to read: "'Meet Lola, the cutest little pony on the planet! And guess what? She's looking for a new home, so some lucky person will get to pet her adorable face every day! Contact the Pet Rescue Club if you want to be that person! Lola can't wait to meet her new best friend!'"

"How does that sound?" Janey asked the others.

"Fine, I guess," Adam said. "I've never had to write an ad for a pony before."

"Yeah." Lolli looked over Zach's shoulder as the first photo appeared below the text. "Anyway, it hardly matters what we write. As soon as people see those pictures, they'll be lining up to take Lola home!"

"Rise and shine, pony girl!"

Lolli cracked one eye open and saw her mother opening her window shades. "What time is it?" she mumbled.

"Time to go out and take care of the pony," her mother replied cheerfully. "You'll have to hurry to get everything done before it's time to leave for school."

"Okay." Lolli yawned and sat up. It felt as if she'd barely slept at all! But she knew Lola needed her, so she dragged herself out of bed and pulled on her clothes.

Lolli woke up a little when Lola spotted her coming and let out her cute high-pitched nicker. The goats and sheep trotted over to

330

say hello, too. Being out with the animals so early in the morning made Lolli feel like a real farmer!

"Good morning, Lola," she said with a smile. "Ready for your breakfast?"

She pulled more hay off the bale and carried it out to the pen. While Lola was eating, Lolli picked up the pony's manure as fast as she could. Luckily there was still plenty of water in the tub, so Lolli figured her friends could help her dump out the leftover water and then scrub and refill the tub after school. By the time she finished everything her arms were tired from picking up manure and scratchy from the hay, and she was pretty sure she didn't smell her best. But there was no time for a shower if she wanted to be on time for school.

"Got to go, Lola," she said, blowing the pony a kiss. "See you this afternoon!"

By the time she arrived at school, Lolli was already yawning. But she felt more alert when Janey rushed over with big news.

"We're getting tons of hits on the blog post about Lola!" Janey reported, holding up her tablet. "See? It's just like I predicted— tons of people want to adopt Lola already!"

"Really?" Lolli smiled, knowing all her hard work that morning had been worth it. "Hooray!"

8

Help from Ms. Tanaka

"Did any more messages come in about Lola?" Lolli asked Janey after school.

The two girls and Zach were waiting for Lolli's father to pick them up. They were going to Lolli's farm to do the afternoon pony chores. Adam was meeting them there after he finished taking care of his afternoon dog-sitting clients.

"Yes—three more since I checked this morning," Janey reported. "Let's read them and see which person sounds the best."

She brought up the first message and scanned it. Lolli was reading over her shoulder.

"Wow," Lolli commented. "I'm not sure this one is serious."

"Yeah," Zach said. "The girl thinks she can keep Lola in her bedroom like a dog or a cat." He laughed. "She must not know how much a little pony can poop!"

"Ew!" Janey made a face at him. "Never mind—here's another one."

She scanned the next message:

I always wanted a pony like Lola! But I need to change her name to Rebel. That's because I'm going to take her to the rodeo and use her to rope cows like a real cowboy. Please write back and tell me when you can bring her to my house. Thanks, Robert.

"Roping cows at the rodeo?" Lolli said. "I don't think Lola would be very good at that!"

"Yeah," Zach said. "Roscoe would be a better rodeo horse than Lola." He laughed. "My cat Mulberry would probably even be better!"

Lolli took the tablet from Janey and scrolled back to the earlier messages, reading over them quickly. "Some of the people who wrote earlier sound okay, at least," she said. "This girl says she has a really big backyard with lots of grass. And this other one says she's ridden ponies at the fair a bunch of times so she knows all about them."

"Okay," Zach said. "So how do we decide who gets her?"

"We'll figure it out," Janey said. "But let's wait a little longer so more people have a chance to see her."

All day Tuesday, Lolli couldn't stop yawning. She and the rest of the Pet Rescue Club went to her farm right after school to take care of Lola. Lolli started pulling some hay off a bale, but she had to stop and yawn three

times in a row.

"Are we keeping you awake?" Zach joked. "Maybe you should take a nap on that hay instead of feeding it to Lola."

"Sorry." Lolli stifled another yawn. "I'm not used to getting up so early every day to do chores."

Adam nodded. "I know what you mean. When I first started dog-walking before school, it was hard to wake up sometimes."

"Never mind," Janey put in. "We got a bunch more messages about Lola today. Some of them sound pretty good."

Zach grinned. "No more rodeo riders?"

"No more rodeo riders." Janey rolled her eyes. "I wrote back to that kid Robert and told him Lola didn't want to be a rodeo pony."

"So how are we going to figure out who

gets to take Lola home?" Lolli asked.

Janey bit her lip. "I'm not sure," she said. "Maybe we should ask Ms. Tanaka for help."

"Our homeroom teacher?" Adam looked surprised. "Why?"

"She told us she used to ride horses when she was younger, remember?" Lolli said. "Asking her is a great idea, Janey!"

She only wished Ms. Tanaka was there to ask right away. Maybe that way Lola could find a home today and Lolli wouldn't have to wake up early again tomorrow!

But when she looked at Lola nibbling her hay, Lolli decided she really didn't mind one more early morning. Not if it meant finding the perfect home for the sweet little pony.

By the time school ended on Wednesday, several more messages had come in about Lola. "Good," Janey told Lolli as the two girls walked outside together. "That way Ms. Tanaka will have plenty to look at. Look, there she is!"

Ms. Tanaka was one of the bus monitors that day. Janey and Lolli waited until she'd finished helping some first graders get on their bus. Then they hurried over and told her what was going on.

"You took in a pony?" Ms. Tanaka looked impressed. "Wow, I didn't realize you kids knew how to take care of horses!"

"We don't," Lolli admitted.

"At least we didn't," Janey added. "We're learning fast."

"Yeah. But we need help figuring out who should get her," Lolli said. "Can you help us? We were hoping you could read the messages and help us figure out who sounds the best."

"Sure, I'll take a look. Just give me a minute to finish up here, okay?" Ms. Tanaka said.

Ten minutes later all the buses were gone and Ms. Tanaka was scanning the messages on Janey's tablet. The more she read, the more worried she looked.

"Oh, dear," she said at last. "To be honest, kids, I'm not sure any of these sound like a good home for a horse—not even a tiny one."

"Really?" Janey's heart sank. "Are you sure?"

"Sorry." Ms. Tanaka scanned the messages again. "Most of these people sound nice and well-meaning, but none of them mention having any experience with horses."

"What about the girl who says she's ridden lots of ponies?" Janey said.

Ms. Tanaka shook her head. "Going on pony rides at the fair isn't the same as taking care of a pony full time," she explained.

"Lola needs a knowledgeable caretaker to keep her healthy and happy."

"But we didn't know anything about taking care of ponies," Janey argued. "And look how great Lola is doing with us!"

"It's only been a couple of days, right?" Ms. Tanaka said gently. "That's not the same as committing to a pony's lifetime."

"Oh." Lolli bit her lip. "So how do we find someone knowledgeable about ponies?"

The teacher scrolled back and read Janey's blog entry. "Well, you might need to adjust your ad a little," she said. "Focus less on how cute Lola is, and more on her needs in a home."

"Okay." Janey sighed. "Could you help me do that?"

Ms. Tanaka smiled. "Sure. But in exchange, you have to let me meet Lola. Okay?"

Janey smiled. "It's a deal!"

"Truman!" Janey cried as a cute little dog jumped out of Ms. Tanaka's car.

The Pet Rescue Club was at the farm again. While waiting for Ms. Tanaka, they'd done the afternoon chores. Lola was eating her hay while Lolli brushed her. Lolli's father was there, too, fixing a piece of the fence that had come loose.

Truman raced over to greet the kids, barking and wagging his tail. Janey hugged him. "I'm glad you brought Truman along," she told Ms. Tanaka, giggling as Truman licked her chin.

Ms. Tanaka smiled. "Truman loves going places," she said. She greeted Mr. Simpson and the other kids. Then she stepped toward the pen. "Oh, you were right—Lola is adorable!"

The pony took one more bite of hay, then wandered over to say hello. Ms. Tanaka scratched Lola's neck, which made her stretch out and grunt happily.

"Hey, she likes that!" Zach exclaimed.

"Horses usually love having their itchy spots scratched," Ms. Tanaka said with a chuckle. She glanced at the pony's hooves. "Oh, dear, it looks as if Lola hasn't had her feet done in quite a while."

"Yeah, Zach's mom said something about that, too," Adam said. "Can you show us how to do it?"

Ms. Tanaka shook her head. "That's a job for an expert," she said. "Lola will need to see a farrier soon—that's another name for a horseshoer, or a blacksmith. She's probably also behind on her shots and deworming, and might even need her teeth floated."

"Floated?" Zach laughed. "Lola's pretty small for a horse, but she's too big to fit in the bathtub!"

Ms. Tanaka laughed, too. "Floating is the term for a horse getting her teeth filed down," she explained. "If it isn't done regularly, her teeth can get sharp and cut her mouth when she tries to eat."

"Oh." Janey bit her lip. "I guess that's not something we can do ourselves, either?"

"No, sorry." The teacher shrugged. "You'll need either a vet or a special horse dentist."

Lolli's father had been listening. "All this is starting to sound expensive," he commented.

"Yes. Keeping a pony isn't cheap." Ms. Tanaka looked sympathetic. She rubbed the pony's shaggy mane and glanced at the kids. "If Lola stays with the Pet Rescue Club much longer, you'll probably need to think about how to raise enough money to pay for her care."

"Yeah." Janey traded an anxious look with her friends.

What had they gotten themselves into?

9

Horsing Around

Lolli could tell that her father was worried about what Ms. Tanaka had said. "It's okay," she said quickly. "We can have a fundraiser. Right, guys?"

"Yeah!" Zach and Janey said at the same time, while Adam nodded.

But Lolli's dad shook his head. "I don't know, kids," he said. "This might be more than we can handle. Lola really needs to be with knowledgeable horse people. We should probably call the shelter in Lakeville— it sounds like they have people there who know how to take care of horses."

"No!" Lolli cried. "We want to help Lola ourselves!"

"Yeah, tons of people have already seen her on the blog," Janey said.

Lolli's dad looked dubious. "But you told me you haven't heard from anyone who sounded right for Lola."

"Ms. T is going to help us write a better ad," Zach told him. "Right, Ms. T?"

Ms. Tanaka was staring thoughtfully at Lola. "I might be able to do better than that," she said. "I just had an idea."

Lolli's heart jumped. "What is it?"

"I just remembered—an old friend of mine keeps her horses at a stable not far from here," the teacher said. "I could call her and see if she'd be willing to help find a new home for Lola."

"Really?" Adam said. "That would be great!"

Janey held her breath while Ms. Tanaka pulled out her cell phone. Just then the goats started head-butting each other and making a lot of noise. Ms. Tanaka stepped away behind the barn where Janey couldn't hear what she was saying.

"Do you think her friend can help?" Lolli wondered, watching as her father waved his hands to shoo the goats away.

"I hope so." Janey gazed at Lola, who was nibbling at some grass beneath the fence. "Because it would be totally vile if Lola had to go to the shelter in Lakeville."

"Yeah," Zach agreed. "Especially after all the work we've been doing!"

A moment later Ms. Tanaka returned. She was smiling. "Good news," she told the kids. "Darby is at the stable right now. She's showing a horse to a potential buyer. But she said we could come on over and she'll talk to us about Lola after she's done."

"What are we waiting for?" Zach exclaimed. "Let's go!"

Ms. Tanaka left Truman at Lolli's house so he could play with Roscoe while they were gone. Then Mr. Simpson drove everyone over in his big old station wagon. On the way, Ms. Tanaka explained that she and Darby had grown up riding together.

"I haven't seen her in a few years, since we're both so busy," she said. "But I heard she's training horses professionally now."

"Just like Adam!" Zach said with a grin. "Only horses instead of dogs."

Mr. Simpson chuckled. "I think we're here."

Janey looked out the window. They were passing a sign for the boarding stable. The driveway curved around some trees and ended by a large riding ring with a pretty green barn beyond. A woman was riding a tall, handsome chestnut horse in the ring.

"Is that her?" Janey asked, squinting at the rider. It was hard to see the woman's face clearly beneath her riding helmet, but she looked at least ten years older than Ms. Tanaka.

"No, Darby's over there, standing by the gate," Ms. Tanaka said, pointing to a woman around her age wearing a baseball cap, tall boots, and sunglasses. "The woman on the horse must be her client."

As soon as they all got out of the car, the younger woman spotted them and waved. "Hi!" she cried, hurrying over to meet them as they reached the ring fence. She gave Ms. Tanaka a big hug. "It's so good to see you! I'm glad you came. We'll be finished here soon."

Ms. Tanaka hugged her back, then introduced everyone. "Don't worry, we'll stay out of your way until you're done," she added.

"No worries," Darby said. "Mrs. Jamison is just trying out this fellow one more time before taking him home."

"What a beautiful horse!" Lolli exclaimed. "Why in the world are you selling him?"

"Lolli!" her father chided. "That's not polite."

Darby laughed. "It's okay," she said. "I'm

selling him because I love helping ex-race-horses find new careers and new people to love them."

"That's a racehorse?" Adam sounded surprised.

Janey was surprised, too. The horse was trotting slowly in a circle, his neck arched proudly. He looked nothing like the lean, fast horses she'd seen racing on TV.

"He used to be a racehorse." Darby smiled as she watched the horse slow to a walk. "Now Red is turning into a wonderful riding horse."

"Red?" Janey could hardly believe her ears. "Did you say that horse's name is Red?"

Zach looked excited. "And he used to be a racehorse?"

Lolli gasped. "I think we know your

horse's best friend!"

Janey, Lolli, Zach, and Adam all started talking at once. Darby looked confused for a second. But when Ms. Tanaka started to explain about Lola, her eyes widened.

"Hang on," she said. "Are you talking about the cute little Shetland pony companion I saw with Red at the track?"

"Yes, that's Lola!" Janey said. "Red's old trainer gave her to some people who couldn't keep her. So now we're trying to find her a home."

Lolli's father nodded. "The trouble is, we're not really equipped to take care of a pony."

"Oh, dear." Darby looked sad. "I wish I could have taken Lola. But I'm not allowed to keep two horses in one stall here, even if one of them is tiny. And the stable is full right now—no extra stalls."

Zach glanced at Red, who was walking past the spot where they were standing. "Do you think Red misses Lola? We heard they were best friends."

Red's rider brought him to a stop. "Hello," she said with a smile. "I couldn't help overhearing some of your conversation...."

"Sorry," Zach said. "I get that a lot. My mom says I'm louder than a howler monkey with a megaphone."

The woman chuckled. "No, it's fine," she said. "But what was that you were saying about Red's best friend?"

Darby repeated what the kids had just

told her. "It seems Lola has lost her home, and these nice kids are trying to find her another one," she said. "I'm hoping I can help."

The woman patted Red. "So this fellow had a pony as a friend? How charming!" She smiled at Janey and the others. "Is there any way I could meet this Lola?"

Together Again

"Of course you can meet Lola!" Janey blurted out.

"She's at Lolli's house," Zach added. "It's only a couple of miles from here."

Lolli nodded. "Maybe you can help us look for a new owner, too!"

"Maybe I can." Mrs. Jamison winked at Darby. "There might not be any extra stalls here, but I happen to have a couple open in my barn at home."

"You have a barn at your house?" Janey

359

asked, feeling a twinge of excitement. "Does that mean you're an experienced horse person?"

Mrs. Jamison laughed. "I like to think I know what I'm doing, at least a little bit."

"Mrs. Jamison is being modest," Darby said with a smile. "She's owned horses all her life—she's as experienced as they come."

"I don't know about that," Mrs. Jamison said. "But I do know I have a couple of young children who might love a tiny equine of their very own."

Janey could hardly believe her ears. Had they just found the perfect new owner for Lola?

"What are we waiting for?" she cried. "Let's go see Lola right now!"

"Calm down, Janey," Lolli's father said with a laugh. "These ladies need to get Red settled back in his stall first."

"Actually, maybe we don't." Mrs. Jamison glanced at Darby. "I wanted to try him out cross-country anyway. Feel like taking a hack?"

"A what?" Janey asked.

"She said a hack." Zach pretended to have a coughing fit.

Darby laughed. "Not that kind of hack," she said. "Hacking is just a horsey word for riding out." She nodded at Mrs. Jamison. "Let me grab a horse and my helmet and we'll go right now."

She hurried into the barn and returned moments later leading a stout brown horse.

"Can you give me a leg up?" she asked Ms. Tanaka.

"Aren't you forgetting something?" Zach asked. "Where's your saddle?"

Ms. Tanaka grinned. "Oh, Darby doesn't need a saddle," she told the kids. "She always did love riding bareback!"

She helped Darby vault onto the horse's back. Then she told her how to get to Lolli's farm.

"Great," Darby said. "We'll meet you there."

"What if they got lost?" Lolli wondered, feeling her stomach flip over with worry. They were so close to finding Lola the perfect home—Lolli didn't want anything to ruin it now!

The Pet Rescue Club, Lolli's father, and Ms. Tanaka were back at Lolli's farm waiting for Darby and Mrs. Jamison to arrive.

"I'm sure they're not lost," Ms. Tanaka said. "Cars are faster than horses, you know."

Zach grinned. "Even racehorses?"

"Even racehorses," Ms. Tanaka replied. "I'm sure they—"

The rest of her words were lost in a loud whinny. Lola had been dozing by the fence while Lolli rubbed her neck. But now the pony raced along the fence, staring out across the driveway.

A second later, another whinny came from that direction. Then Red and Mrs.

Jamison came into view. Red was trotting toward the Pet Rescue Club with his ears pricked forward. Darby and her horse were right behind him.

"It looks like we found the right place," Mrs. Jamison called. "At least Red seems to recognize his friend!"

Lola started running back and forth on her side of the fence, whinnying and snorting. Janey had never seen her move so fast!

"Look—Lola thinks she's a racehorse, too," Zach joked.

Lolli couldn't respond. She was too busy watching as Red reached the pen. Mrs. Jamison let the reins go loose, and Red stretched his long neck over the fence, nuzzling at Lola. She stretched up, nuzzling him back.

"Well," Mrs. Jamison said with a smile. "I suppose this settles it. Lola will just have to come home with me and Red."

"Really?" Janey gasped. "That's awesome!"

"Yes, it is." Darby was smiling, too. "And to celebrate the happy occasion, I'll throw in some free training for Lola. I'm sure we can turn her into the perfect little riding pony for Mrs. Jamison's kids."

"Hooray!" Zach cheered.

"The Pet Rescue Club did it again," Janey exclaimed.

Adam grinned at Ms. Tanaka and Darby. "With a little help from our friends," he added. "Thanks, Ms. Tanaka!"

"I'm happy to help." The teacher winked. "After all, I owe you one. Without the Pet Rescue Club, I wouldn't have my Truman!"

Just then there was a flurry of excited barking from the direction of the house. Lolli's mother appeared, with Truman and Roscoe pulling at their leashes.

Meanwhile, Janey was still watching the happy reunion between Red and Lola. "We'll miss you, Lola," she said.

"Yeah," Lolli added. "But I won't miss

getting up at the crack of dawn to feed you."

Zach grinned. "And I won't miss flinging horse poo around."

"If you do, you can always come by my barn to help clean stalls," Mrs. Jamison told him with a chuckle. She glanced around at all the kids. "And I hope you'll all come by to visit Lola."

"Definitely," Janey promised.

Lolli's father smiled. "All's well that ends well," he said. "But maybe the Pet Rescue Club should stick to dogs and cats from now on."

Zach grinned. "We can't make any promises," he joked.

"May I borrow your phone?" Lolli asked her mother. "I want to call the shelter and let Kitty know we found a perfect home for Lola."

"Of course." Mrs. Simpson fished her cell phone out of her pocket and handed it over.

Soon Lolli was talking to the shelter worker. Kitty was thrilled by the news about Lola. "Congratulations," she said. "But Lolli, I was just going to call you."

"You were? Was it about Lola?" Lolli asked.

"No, it's about the rabbit you saw the other day," Kitty said. "Someone wants to adopt him. It's a lady who has kept house rabbits all her life and saw our bunny's listing online. But since you said you might want to adopt the little guy, I thought I should check in first and see if you're still interested."

Lolli hesitated, remembering how soft and sweet the bunny was. Then she shook her head.

"Thanks for asking," she said. "But actually, taking care of Lola made me realize I might not be the best home for a rabbit after all. And that lady sounds perfect."

"I see." Kitty sounded impressed. "All right, then. The lady will be very happy!"

Lolli hung up and turned around to see Janey staring at her. "Was that about the bunny?" Janey sounded disappointed. "Are you sure you don't want to adopt him?"

Lolli stepped over to pet Roscoe. "I don't really need another pet right now," she said. She glanced at Lola and Red. "Not when there are so many animals out there who need my time and energy to find them homes."

"True." Janey smiled at her. "They definitely need you—and the rest of the Pet Rescue Club!"

Pony Prep

Are you ready for a horse or pony of your own? Or would a different kind of pet suit your lifestyle better? Take this quiz and find out!

Where do you live?

A) On a farm

B) In a suburban house with a yard

C) In a city apartment or condo

How much time can you spend with your new pet?

A) Lots of time—my pet is my hobby!

B) An hour or so per day

C) Only a little bit—I'm super busy!

How would you describe yourself?

A) I'm not afraid of hard work and getting dirty.

B) I love to play games and run around outside.

C) I like to relax, be comfortable, and keep my hands clean.

How much experience have you had with horses or ponies?

A) Tons of hands-on experience—I've taken riding lessons and/or worked on a horse farm.

B) Some experience—I've been on a trail ride, read lots of books about horses, and/or watched plenty of movies or videos about them.

C) Nothing—I don't know which end of the horse whinnies!

Results

Mostly *A*s: If your answers were all or mostly *A*, congratulations! You just might be ready for pony ownership!

Mostly *B*s: If your answers were all or mostly *B*, you might not be quite ready for a pony yet. Going on trail rides and reading books are good ways to learn, but you'll want to get more experience before you take the pony plunge. Ask your parents if you can take riding lessons to learn even more. In the meantime, your lifestyle might be better suited for a lively dog, puppy, or kitten!

Mostly *C*s: If your answers were all or mostly *C*, you probably don't even want a pony. They require lots of knowledge and work—and some of that work can get you pretty dirty! You might get along better with a quiet adult cat, a tank of fish, or another smaller, less active pet.

Luckily, there are pets out there for all kinds of people! Check out the ASPCA website (*www.aspca.org*) for more tips on caring for horses and pets of all types.

The Real Lola

Lola the homeless pony was inspired by a real-life animal rescue story. A famous show-jumping rider was at a big show, where she happened to meet a miniature horse (another kind of small equine) named Lola. When she found out that Lola had been headed to slaughter—and that she had a young foal—the rider decided to adopt them both! The real-life Lola and her son, Harley, now live happily on the rider's farm, where Harley is learning to be a tiny riding horse for the rider's young son.